a *Line of Duty* novel

ASKING
For Trouble

a Line of Duty novel

ASKING for Trouble

#1 *NEW YORK TIMES* BESTSELLING AUTHOR
TESSA BAILEY

This book is a work of fiction. Names, characters, places, and incidents are the product of the author's imagination or are used fictitiously. Any resemblance to actual events, locales, or persons, living or dead, is coincidental.

Copyright © 2013 by Tessa Bailey. All rights reserved, including the right to reproduce, distribute, or transmit in any form or by any means. For information regarding subsidiary rights, please contact the Publisher.

Entangled Publishing, LLC
644 Shrewsbury Commons Ave
STE 181
Shrewsbury, PA 17361
rights@entangledpublishing.com

Brazen is an imprint of Entangled Publishing, LLC.

Edited by Heather Howland and Liz Pelletier
Cover design by LJ Anderson/Mayhem Cover Creations
Cover photography by Vitalik Radko/Depositphotos

Manufactured in the United States of America

First Edition November 2013

*To my cousins J & J
For teaching me the art of the insult*

Chapter One

If he winks at me one more time, I'm going to introduce his nuts to my size seven stiletto.

Hayden Winstead circled her ankle slowly underneath the bottle-laden table, barely repressing the urge to follow through on that visually satisfying thought. With three glasses of wine humming through her veins, it seemed like a reasonable way to wipe the patronizing smirk off Brent Mason's face. Knowing Brent, however, needling her until she snapped was his goal, so she'd be damned before giving him an ounce of satisfaction.

The first time they'd met, in this very pub, he'd hit on her using so little finesse, she'd been forced to ask if he was kidding. Granted, they'd both had a few too many drinks that night, but nothing excused the line, "I'm not drunk, I'm just intoxicated by you." *Nothing.*

Especially in light of what he said upon bringing her home and seeing where she lived. *Ah, now I get it. You only date men in certain zip codes.* His comment about her Upper West Side town house still rankled months later. Which is why she'd never regretted her own saccharine-sweet response. *Speaking of zip codes, shouldn't you be getting back to yours? Or is the zoo already closed for the night?*

That's where their acquaintance had begun. From there, it had gone downhill fast.

Really, they should have never been required to share the same oxygen ever again. Life would have been so much easier that way. Too bad their best friends, Daniel and Story, happened to be disgustingly in love. The kind of love that required them to be together practically nonstop, forcing Hayden into Brent's presence with nauseating frequency.

Case in point, tonight. They all sat in their local hangout, Quincy's, waiting for Story to return from her first day of work. An outing that put Hayden across from three unavailable men wearing her best damn underwear. *Pathetic.* A lot of women might have already removed said panties and flung them at their choice of the three NYPD Emergency Service officers. Men in uniform, and all that business.

Hayden's were staying put.

Daniel Chase, hostage negotiator and former love-'em-and-leave-'em guru, was Story's boyfriend and therefore strictly off-limits. As if he could even see anyone besides Hayden's best friend. To Daniel's right, staring pensively into his beer, sat former military sniper Matt Donovan. Not technically unavailable, but quiet and mysterious enough to give a girl the shivers.

Then there was Brent, explosives expert, or as he referred to himself, "blower-up of shit." The man in question took a long pull of his beer, watching her the entire time. His confidence that very first night had irked her more than anything. Sure, a six-foot-five police officer built like a brick shithouse probably didn't get turned down very often by women. Daniel might be the smooth, almost-beautiful one, but Brent had a rough-and-tumble quality to him that Hayden imagined drew women like bees to honey. With full, dark-blond hair and moss-green eyes, he couldn't be described as classically handsome. More like a rugged sailor left over from a different time. The kind of man who picked up a woman in Times Square upon returning from war and threw her over his shoulder to take home to bed.

And that's my cue to stop drinking.

Brent saluted her with his beer bottle. "What are you thinking about over there, duchess? Whatever it is looks mighty interesting."

Her smile almost cracked upon hearing the infuriating nickname he refused to drop. "If I thought you had even a remote chance of keeping up, I'd tell you."

"That so?" He leaned forward on his elbows, not stopping to acknowledge Matt's irritated sigh. "Let's see if I can guess."

"Please do." She took a dainty sip of her white wine. "Knock me over with your sparkling intellect."

He stroked his chin. "There's only so many things it could be. Planning your next fancy cocktail party, trying to remember if you made that *crucial* hair appointment—"

Daniel elbowed Brent in the ribs, giving them both a stern look. "Could you two give it a rest for one night? I've got enough on my mind."

"Like what?" she and Brent asked at the same time, before exchanging a glare.

Daniel opened his mouth to explain, then shook his head, shooting another anxious glance at the entrance to Quincy's. "Nothing."

"Aw, I know what it is." Brent clapped a hand onto Daniel's shoulder. "You're worried how Story's first day went. You're afraid she's going to vamoose back to California."

"No shit," Matt muttered.

"I should have met her at the damn school and walked her here." Daniel ran impatient fingers through his hair, the cool facade he always kept in place beginning to slip. "She has a terrible sense of direction."

"Do you want me to call her?" Hayden offered.

Brent shook his head before Daniel could respond. "Nah, just let her quit that horrible job in peace. Then we'll all go help her pack."

Hayden sent him a withering look, already formulating what she'd say to him when they were alone. Over the last two months, she'd become acquainted with the ball-breaking dynamic between the guys, but when it came to Story, Daniel had always been particularly vulnerable. When the two met in July, she'd only been planning on staying in New York for a couple weeks before returning to her home in California. Now that their relationship had progressed, she had no intention of going back, but Daniel still spent every free moment making sure she never regretted her decision to quit the teaching job she loved and move three thousand miles to be with him.

She tried once more to comfort Daniel. "You know Story. She probably stopped to pet every puppy between here and the school. She's easily distracted."

Daniel leaned back in his chair, eyelids drooping a little, transforming before her eyes into the playboy he resembled. "Don't I know it?"

Satisfied that she'd taken his mind off the possibility her best friend hated her new job, Hayden took another sip of wine and continued to ignore Brent's unwavering gaze. She hated it when he did this. Fixated on her and refused to look away. He looked like a hungry wolf stalking a lamb. As though he also couldn't wait for the opportunity to tell her once again how pampered and pointless he found her posh, Upper West Side lifestyle.

Daniel, all restless energy once again, hopped up from the table. "You guys want another drink? I'm buying."

"I'll come with you," Matt said, shooting a knowing look

between Brent and Hayden.

The second Daniel and Matt moved out of earshot toward the bar, Hayden's glass *clunked* down on the table. "Could you try just a *pinch* harder to be less of a spectacular asshole? He's worried enough. You don't need to make it worse with your douche-bag sorcery."

"*I'm* making it worse? Why don't you sew his name into his underwear and send him off to summer camp?" He tilted his head. "Not all of us had nannies growing up. Some of us can take care of ourselves."

She felt her neck flush as the barb struck home, but she refused to let her reaction show on her face. It would be a cold day in hell before she let him know how much being summed up as a helpless socialite bothered her. "There's a time and a place for insults. Learn the difference, dickhead."

Brent leaned across the table, his jaw tight. "I don't need lessons on how to talk to my friend."

"Disagree. I think you need lessons on quite a few things."

If she'd blinked, she would have missed the telltale tic in his cheek, a sign she'd come to recognize as his temper stirring. Brent might be lacking in polite social skills and empathy, but he made up for it in pride. "Yeah? And who's going to teach me those lessons? You?"

His expression transformed with the sensual challenge, and he drawled the final word with such skepticism, her spine went rigid. Dammit, he *always* made it sexual. He knew it shut her down. Forced her to back off. She could throw around insults with the best of them—just not about sex. Though she was far from a blushing virgin, she'd never hit her stride in that department. When she dated, it was usually to keep her mother off her back. The dates very rarely ended up in bed. And if they *did* end up "shaking the sheets," it frequently ended in disappointment.

Hayden couldn't quite put her finger on what she needed.

She just knew she needed *more*. Not love. No, no. Nor did she want polite sex. Or affectionate sex. She needed something… else.

"What's wrong, rich girl?" Brent grinned and sipped his beer. "Afraid you'd like it too much?"

"No," she responded a little too quickly. "I'm afraid *you* would like it too much and I'd never get rid of your lumbering ass."

Hayden's mouth snapped shut. It was the first time she'd ever responded to one of his endless sexual innuendos in kind. She tried not to panic when he did an interested double take.

"Is that right?"

She raised her chin in response, frowning when his gaze briefly landed on her lips.

"How…*exactly*…would you make me like it, duchess?"

A sarcastic brush-off sat poised on the tip of her tongue, but she held it back. This game had gotten old and he'd grown too sure of himself. A new idea began to formulate in her mind. One Brent wouldn't see coming. She'd call his bluff. He insisted on turning their arguments sexual to quiet her down? He didn't think the spoiled debutante could keep up? Well, this time she'd see just how far he was willing to take the game. Not far, she guessed. Hoped. The idea of voluntarily touching each other had to be just as abhorrent to him. Which is exactly what she wanted.

Tonight, they'd finally declare a winner of this ongoing battle of wits and wills.

When she unbuttoned the top two buttons on her shirt and let the material gape, Brent's beer bottle froze halfway to his mouth. His Adam's apple bobbed a little as he glimpsed her exposed flesh. *That's right, I'm wearing my best matching underwear set, sucker. And I'm finished backing down.*

Her voice dropped to a seductive purr. "It would be so

much more fun to *show* you."

...

Well, I'll be damned. She's not completely *made of ice.*

Brent tried not to be obvious as he shifted in his seat to accommodate the swelling flesh between his legs. Unfortunately, tonight didn't mark the first occasion Her Highness had made him so hard he couldn't sit still. It did, however, mark the first occasion she'd done it intentionally.

Across the table, her eyes issued an unmistakable challenge. What the hell was her game? Any other night, she would have turned her pert little nose up at his baiting question and given him her patented ice-princess frown. Something was definitely up.

Since the night they met, the two of them had mixed about as well as orange juice and toothpaste. He rigged explosives for the NYPD Emergency Service Unit. She flitted about all day organizing charity functions and dinner parties for Manhattan's elite. He lived in a blue-collar neighborhood in Queens. She lived in a massive town house in one of the wealthiest parts of the city. He wore jeans and T-shirts. She wore tight, knee-length skirts and expensive blouses. If the circumstances were different, she would never share a table with him.

That was the part that got to him the most. Every word out of her mouth, every haughty glance in his direction, was designed to let him know she had better things to do. Better *people* to spend her time with.

Then there were those fucking stockings. The thing about her that drove him absolutely crazy. An anomaly he couldn't figure out. From her perfectly styled chocolate-brown hair down to her knees, she looked prim and proper. Like she spent hours at the gym, all the while refusing to give anyone a peek of what all that hard work had yielded. But that careful polish ended with her legs. Tonight, tightly woven fishnet stockings disappeared up underneath her skintight gray skirt. Other days, she wore sheer black tights with a thick line running down the backs of her calves. Frankly, it infuriated him that she couldn't just stick to one look. Die-hard prude or closet sex kitten. Which was it?

His mind drifted back to the gauntlet she'd just tossed down on the table. *It would be so much more fun to show you.* If she thought he wouldn't accept her challenge, she was in for a huge surprise. If for no other reason, he'd swallow his dislike of her for a chance to mess up her artfully coiffed hair. There *was* another reason, however. Hayden might irritate him at every turn, but damn if he didn't spend an inordinate amount of time wondering what it'd be like to have her beneath him. All that holier-than-thou hostility channeled into something productive for once.

Oh yeah, he'd love the chance to pound out this ridiculous, inconvenient attraction for someone he didn't even like. Maybe then he could stop fantasizing about her every time they were in the same room. Picturing her bent over his dining room table in her stockings. *Only* her stockings. Giving him that look that said *I've been such a bad girl, Brent.*

When he didn't answer her question right away, he saw her confidence falter. Yup, definitely up to something. Bluffing him? Maybe she thought it would be funny to get the non-Ivy League-educated roughneck hot and bothered, then prance out of the bar, leaving him with an epic cockstand. *Not going to happen, baby.*

Well, the epic cockstand was unavoidable, but at least it would be on his terms.

"What exactly is your idea of *showing* me, duchess?" He smirked. "Silk sheets, candlelight…the gentle strains of Kenny G. I'd love to see how the other half fucks."

Something flared behind her eyes as she sat straighter in her chair. Brent barely had the willpower to keep his eyes off her breasts as they pressed snugly against her blouse, putting her smooth cleavage on display for him. When her tongue skated across her lips, leaving them glistening, he swallowed hard. "On second thought, who doesn't love a little saxophone in the bedroom?"

Hayden's finger slid through the condensation on the side of her wineglass. "How do you know?"

"Know what?"

Her eyelids drew up slowly as if weighed down by arousal. "How do you know we'll even make it to the bedroom?"

His mouth went dry. "Come again?"

"That would be the plan."

As soon as the heat-inducing words left her mouth, Daniel and Matt returned with their round of drinks. Brent wanted to growl at his friends' shitty timing. He and Hayden both retreated, him reluctantly leaning back in his chair, Hayden crossing those mysterious legs. *Damn.* Just how far was she willing to take this game? He might not like her, he might resent the hell out of her superior attitude, but he'd sure as hell love to find out once and for all what lay at the top of those stockings. No way would she let him get that far, though. Wouldn't want his dirty, workingman's hands on her perfectly toned thighs.

Would she?

Daniel's chair scraped back, snapping him out of his thoughts. "She's here."

"Thank God," he and Hayden muttered at the same time, followed by a mutual eye-roll.

Brent stood, unable to stop his sigh of relief when he saw Story walking toward them wearing a huge smile and waving in their direction. Daniel lifted her into a bear hug, then sat her down on his lap. Two months later, Brent could still hardly believe how fast and hard his womanizing best friend had fallen. If he wasn't so damn happy for the guy, he would have groaned at the way Daniel couldn't stop staring at the sunny, fedora-wearing blonde perched on his lap.

"You guys like the hat I bought on the way here?" Story looked between the guys and Hayden. "Am I hat girl?"

Hayden tilted her head. "You could definitely be hat girl. I'd like to see more options, though. Top hat, beanie…maybe the kind with the spinner on top?"

"A Mets hat," Brent interjected.

Story laughed and stroked the back of Daniel's neck. "So what are we doing tonight? Mexican food? I could drink my weight in sangria—"

Daniel shook his head, "My place."

"Already? I just got here." Story looked surprised, but when Daniel whispered something against her ear, she took a shaky breath and nodded. "Your place it is."

"Brent, Matt, can you—" Daniel started.

"Don't worry." Brent gave Hayden a slow grin. "I'll make sure Ms. Winstead gets home."

Daniel didn't wait for a response, taking Story's hand and dragging her from the bar.

"Bye, guys!" Story called over her shoulder.

Hayden gave her friend a halfhearted salute, then refocused on Brent. "I'm not letting you drive me anywhere. You've been drinking."

Brent held up the bottle so she could see the label. "Nonalcoholic." He barely contained his laughter when her chin only went up another notch. "I don't drink during the week."

"Lucky me," she said under her breath.

"That would be the plan."

Hayden's eyes widened as he tossed her words back in her face, right in front of Matt.

Matt not-so-discreetly checked his watch. "Damn, would you look at the time?" He pushed back his chair, then followed in Daniel and Story's wake. "Try not to kill each other. I like this place."

"You ready to call it a night, too?" Brent picked up his fresh beer and winked at Hayden. "Or do you want to keep going?"

"Call it a night?" She tossed her hair back over one shoulder. "We're only getting started."

Chapter Two

For the first time in history, she and Brent were alone. Voluntarily, that is. Normally at this stage, they would flee each other's presence without bothering to make an excuse. Unless you counted a certain obscene gesture as an excuse.

Hayden's pulse accelerated as Brent rose to his full height and rounded the table to occupy the chair beside her. Why were her palms sweating? They were only playing a game. Any minute now, Brent would give in and she'd be free to strut out of Quincy's, reveling in her victory. That hot look in his eye, the one that continued to dip and linger on her exposed neckline, was all for show.

Right?

When he draped an arm over the back of her chair and leaned in close, she ignored the flutter in her stomach. It had to be the wine. Brent Mason did *not* give her flutters. He only gave her hives.

"So tell me," he started, his voice taking on a deeper tone. "Assuming we didn't make it to your professionally decorated bedroom, how far would we make it?"

She doused a flare of annoyance. He never let her forget her status, not for a second. Or that she'd done so little to earn it. "Something tells me a man like you can't hold out long enough to make it past the entryway. Just wham-bam, let me get back to playing *Grand Theft Auto*, ma'am."

"I prefer *Halo*," Brent said in a tight voice. "And let's be honest. The real reason you don't want me in your bed is because I'll sully your lily-white sheets."

Okay, that stung a little. It had been a while since her sheets were sullied, but he didn't know that. His comment proved he thought of her as a cold fish, too focused on appearances to feel anything, sexually or otherwise. Especially for a man without an exorbitant bank account.

No way would she back down now. It would have to be him.

It suddenly became clear how to accomplish that end. A caveman like Brent would need to be the aggressor in bed, no doubt. She would lay odds that he would cling to that macho image with both hands. Hayden almost laughed out loud. He wouldn't be able to cling on to much of anything with both hands secured behind his back.

She turned in her chair, letting her knee rub along the inside of Brent's thigh, doing an internal fist-pump when he sucked in a breath. "That's not it at all, Brent. I just don't like waiting." Garnering her courage, she dragged her fingers up the inside of his arm. "You wouldn't happen to have your handcuffs handy, would you?"

He dragged his heated gaze away from her fingers. "If you like being cuffed, I have no problem accommodating you, baby."

"Actually," she returned, drawing the word out, "I was thinking I would cuff *you*."

She held her breath. Any minute now, he'd scoff at her request and this charade would be over. Funny, she wasn't quite as ready to walk away as she had been moments ago. In fact, the thought of Brent's big body, restrained by handcuffs, was surprisingly appealing. That fluttering in her stomach had graduated into a constant tug, confusing her further.

"Done." Hayden hid her shock as Brent leaned close and spoke gruffly near her ear. "Be warned, though. If you take away the use of my hands, I'll only make up for it with my mouth."

"R-really?" Her voice sounded breathy to her own ears. It simply wasn't possible that Brent was turning her on. She shouldn't have drunk so much wine without eating a proper dinner. That was the only explanation for her body's potent reaction to Brent's words.

"Why does that surprise you, duchess?" His expression turned patronizing, but she could still see the desire kindling in his eyes, the way they fixated on her mouth. "You think because I don't wear a suit to work, I haven't learned how to pleasure a woman?"

A punch of heat reverberated through her system, layered on top of the indignation brought on by his jab. He couldn't mean it. He didn't give a damn about her pleasure. No, they were both simply playing the game. When it came time to put the handcuffs on, he would back down. No way would he put himself at his enemy's mercy. "I guess we'll find out if you're capable of shutting up long enough to use your mouth for something worthwhile."

"Will we?" He gripped her knees in his hands. "You going to uncross these sexy thighs long enough to find out what I can do between them?"

As her heart began to pound out of control, it occurred to her that she might lose this battle. Brent didn't appear any closer to caving, and they were drawing dangerously close to the end of the line. This conversation couldn't continue in its current vein much longer without them leaving together.

Judging from his expression, he still expected her to cry uncle. Clearly skeptical of her ability to follow through.

Time for a change of strategy.

She uncrossed her legs and stood, putting her breasts just beneath his line of vision. When his confident smile slipped a little, she swallowed a triumphant laugh. "I'm tired of talking about it." Her fingers slipped through his hair and clutched tight. "Put up or shut up, big boy."

"Big boy." When Brent stood, his hard body dragged slowly over her curves, catching Hayden's breath in her throat. "You have no idea. Think you can handle me?"

Could she handle him? He didn't look like the type to be *handled* by anyone. Least of all her, who could count her sexual partners on one carefully manicured hand. At least if it got that far—which it surely wouldn't—she'd have a much easier time *handling* him if he didn't have the use of his hands.

Throat tight and unable to issue a verbal response, Hayden turned and walked toward the exit in lieu of answering out loud. Brent's heavy tread followed purposefully behind her, sending a shiver up her spine. With each step toward the door, she grew less and less sure of whether anticipation or nerves were the culprit.

They rode in silence on the crosstown drive from Quincy's, although the tense atmosphere in Brent's SUV spoke volumes. Her decision-making window was rapidly closing. It had been incredibly easy to talk a big game while sitting in Quincy's. Now, however, her bravado was beginning to wane.

She let her gaze slide across the center console to inspect the man taking up well over his fair share of the SUV. Powerful thighs flexed beneath the steering wheel as he applied the brake. Defined arm muscles shifted as he took a right turn. His shoulders were so broad they bridged the console and nearly touched her own.

Most infuriating of all, a cocky, knowing smile played around his lips like he expected her to back out at any minute. If she admitted to bluffing him now, he would never let her live it down. She'd be doomed to see that shit-eating grin every time they met. Nope. Couldn't let it happen. One way or another, the big guy was going down.

He eased his SUV to a stop outside Hayden's town house and she pushed open the passenger-side door. "Are you coming in? Or are you afraid of losing he-man status by being cuffed by a girl?"

Brent's forearm brushed her thighs as he reached for the glove compartment and popped it open. Hayden felt a simultaneous surge of arousal and panic when a silver pair of handcuffs were revealed. "One question. Is flash photography allowed on this ride?"

"Not unless you want a bloody stump for a hand."

An amused smile lit his face. "I think in a matter of minutes, you're going to be very glad I still have both hands. You might even change your mind about using those handcuffs."

Her first instinct dictated she throw herself out of the vehicle and run screaming toward her house. Lock herself inside and watch reruns of *The Facts of Life*. But then an image of a shirtless Brent kneeling, hands cuffed behind his back, materialized in her mind. She felt another jolt of surprise when lust, hot and insistent, pooled in her tummy. In addition to shocking her, the heady response bred irritation. She hadn't experienced the feeling in a long time, and the fact that her nemesis provoked it in her chafed.

Too late to turn back now.

"I won't be changing my mind." Hayden stuffed the handcuffs into her purse. "It's too bad the NYPD doesn't issue ball gags in addition to handcuffs," she said, smiling brightly. "Not that your voice isn't a seductive lullaby."

"I haven't had any complaints."

"Then consider this your first." Hayden exited the SUV, her heels *tapping* along the sidewalk. As she ascended the stone stairs leading to her front door, she felt him following behind her. She scanned the surrounding area, looking for her parents, who lived in the same neighborhood. If they saw her entering her town house with this swaggering hulk of a male, they would surely have some questions.

"Worried about being seen with me?" His jaw tightened and flexed. "Don't worry, I'm sure your little lesson won't take long."

The jerk still thought she would back down from her own challenge. "It's going to be over that fast, huh? Don't worry, champ. It's a very common problem among men. Happens to the best of them."

She could practically feel the steam shooting from his ears. Smiling to herself, Hayden pushed the front door open and entered the dark foyer. The second the door closed behind her, Brent pushed her up against it, bracing himself with both arms on the door. Never having been this close to him before, she took a moment to absorb the jarring differences between them. His body, so incredibly hard and well-built, pressed against her softer, smaller frame. At least a foot taller than her, he would have to bend his knees to kiss her…or pick her up for their mouths to meet. Something needy shivered through her at the thought of him using all that strength on her. Even more tempting was the thought of leashing that power. Tempting it out of him.

"You're testing my patience here, duchess," he growled. "If you have any doubt about my ability to fuck the ever-loving sarcasm right out of you, I'll be more than happy to clear it up."

Hayden sucked in a breath. Until now, they'd been dancing around any talk of the main event, but he'd just put it in black-and-white terms. Was she willing to let it get that far? This wouldn't be the kind of one-night stand you walked away from unscathed. If they took it to that level, she would be forced to see the knowledge of what they'd done written all over his arrogant face every time they were wrangled into spending time together.

"What's wrong? Is this lesson you're attempting to teach me over before it even began?" Patronizing laughter rumbled in his big chest. His hips pressed closer and she could feel his thick arousal. "Too bad. I thought I was finally going to solve the mystery tonight."

"What mystery is that?" she asked against her better judgment.

"I've been wondering what it'll take to wipe that self-satisfied expression off your face." He bent down, let his mouth hover an inch above hers. "What gets you off, rich girl? Besides a shoe sale."

With their bodies molded together, she ached for something she couldn't name, his words burrowed even further under her skin. He found her vapid. Trivial. He thought she took her wealth for granted, when in reality, she spent every day of her life trying to deserve it. Prove herself worthy. And oftentimes...coming up short. He didn't think she had the ability to feel anything? The need to prove him wrong, right then and there, shook Hayden to the soles of her feet. Her purse hit the floor with a thud.

She pushed higher on her toes, fusing her mouth to his. Brent's body jerked, making her feel exultant. She'd caught him off guard. Her fingers wove their way through his hair and tugged hard to bring him closer. They nipped at each other's lips, testing, seeking. He grazed her jaw with his teeth before returning to her mouth to taste her with thorough licks of his tongue, spiking heat through Hayden. Her hands dropped to his waist and urged him forward, wordlessly begging him to rub his erection against her belly. When he did so, once, twice, they both broke away on a groan. For a single second, they locked eyes, as if to say *oh shit*. Involuntarily, her attention dropped to his arousal, heavy and insistent between them.

Brent kept his gaze on her face as he worked himself against her. "I'll let you ride it, duchess. And I'm going to keep your tongue busy in my mouth the whole time." With one hand, he stripped his shirt off over his head, revealing his massive chest and rock-hard muscles. "That ought to keep the sarcasm at bay for a couple hours."

Hayden shoved against him, but he didn't budge. "What's going to keep your ego at bay?" she asked through clenched teeth. "One more crack like that and you can go home to your bachelor pad and *self-satisfy* until the sun comes—"

He claimed her mouth once again on a growl. A single forearm curled under her bottom and lifted with so little effort, her thoughts went fuzzy, blurring her indignation into nothingness. His mouth moved, rough and demanding over hers, forcing her lips wide to receive rhythmic thrusts from his tongue. Hayden could only twine her arms around his neck and hold on as white-hot need poured through her in waves. She made a sound of protest in his mouth when she couldn't get her lower body close enough. A throb drummed between her thighs and she ached to feel pressure there. When she communicated her desire for friction with a twist of her hips, he tried to wedge his hips between her thighs, but the tight material of her skirt wouldn't allow it.

"Take it off, Hayden, or I rip it off."

Brent's rasped command at her neck brought her back down to earth. Just a little. If she took off her skirt, he would take her against the door. *Wham-bam, Grand Theft Auto, ma'am*. He'd whistle his way out the door, knowing exactly who had *handled* whom. Next time she saw him, he'd give her one of his signature winks and tell her to call him next time she needed a ride. She couldn't let that happen. She'd instigated this for a reason. To show him how little he actually knew about her. To put a dent in his overblown ego. She needed to get the upper hand back. Now.

Hayden broke their kiss, let the corners of her lips edge into a sensual smile. "I think it's about time we broke out those handcuffs."

Brent's hands moved down her back to mold her bottom with rough palms. "Patience, duchess. I haven't gotten my fill of touching you yet." He boosted her higher against the door. "Before I let you restrain me, I'm going to make damn sure you're too revved up to stop."

His mouth seized hers once more. This time, she could feel more urgency behind the kiss, reflected in the rigid lines of his body. It only drove her need higher. Clinging to his shoulders, she let his frenzied mouth slant over hers several times. She broke away with a moan, her resolve slipping drastically under the onslaught of sensations. If she could just get the handcuffs on him, she could stop him from overwhelming her.

"You're right," she whispered. "We should have some fun first." She dropped to her knees. Let her hands wander up those muscular thighs.

Above her, Brent's breathing deepened, kicked up into a faster pace. "Only for a little while. Then I find out what's beneath that skirt."

With a dutiful nod, she unbuttoned his fly. Even nuzzled her cheek against his rigid erection and smiled when he sucked in a quick breath. He laced his fingers through her hair and tilted his hips toward her mouth. "Uh-uh," she admonished. "No touching."

"Sure, baby." He put his hands behind his back and closed his eyes. "If that's the way you like it."

As soon as his hands crossed behind him, she carefully

slipped the handcuffs from her purse and slapped them onto his wrists. Hearing his low curse, she gained her feet, taking a moment to savor the sight of him, all that commanding power harnessed. By her. "Looks like somebody just got handled."

"Take them off," he ground out. "I'm not done with you yet."

Hayden pretended to consider the idea. "Hmm. No."

Brent cursed under his breath. "So what's your evil plan? Take blackmail photos to amuse your simpering friends at your next themed tea party?"

"Tea parties are very last season. Try to keep up." She sauntered forward, walking him backward with gentle nudges of her hand until he fell back onto the cushioned bench placed along the far wall of the foyer. He gave her a look of warning, one she'd never seen on his face before. It gave her momentary pause, but did nothing to sway her intentions. Using his broad shoulders for balance, she straddled him on the bench, remaining standing on her knees and putting her breasts at eye level.

Hayden could see his anger battling with arousal. But he kept his pissed-off gaze resolutely on her face. Until she started unbuttoning her blouse. Picking up where she'd left off at the bar, she popped each button out slowly, methodically, until she had his rapt attention. His throat worked as he swallowed heavily, tongue licking out to wet his lips with each inch of skin she revealed. Power surged through Hayden. She had two hundred and fifty pounds of rugged male between her legs. And she had complete control. She drew her unbuttoned blouse over her shoulders and let it fall to the floor, leaving her in a crimson lace bra.

"I've got news for you," he rasped, eyes blazing. "Seeing your breasts is not the worst form of punishment."

"It will be," she said huskily, undoing the front hook of her bra. "Because seeing them is all you get. And, Brent?"

She kissed him fast and hard. "I've got a fabulous pair. So that's really going to suck for you."

Hayden parted the crimson material and revealed her breasts. Brent made a strangled noise and lurched forward on the bench, as though he couldn't restrain himself. She dodged his mouth at the last second, staving him off with two hands on his shoulders. Still, he didn't look away from her naked chest, mouth working as if he could already taste her. His unchecked reaction made hunger spread through her system like fire. Gone was the cocky son of a bitch she'd come to know. He looked like a starving man eyeing his last meal.

"Scoot forward," he asked in a gravelly voice. "Just a little. I promise I'll suck them so good for you. So good."

His words enticed her like mad. It would be so easy to pretend the conflict between them didn't exist and they were simply two people who desperately needed pleasure. She *needed* his mouth on her, she realized. Tempting him beyond control would be more difficult than she thought. In the process, she herself was being tempted. *Don't give him the satisfaction of knowing how thoroughly he's affecting you.*

Hayden took a deep breath and shook her head. "Sorry, big boy. Not going to happen." She gave in to the impulse to tease his neck with a kiss, but he turned his head at the last second and caught her mouth. This kiss felt different. Persuasive, entreating. As if he'd finally started taking this encounter seriously. It made her desperate to squeeze her legs together, but they were spread wide on either side of his hips. When she heard herself moan low in her throat, she broke away.

Between them, her nipples pouted, begging for Brent's attention. Before she could stop him, he leaned forward and sucked one into his mouth, rolling it on his tongue and groaning. Then he pulled back just a little and blew on it gently. Hayden's eyelids drooped, her lips parted. She felt each sensual movement of his tongue in every secret place on her body. His gaze met hers, looking for any sign of protest. He seemed to know how close she was to caving because when he spoke, his dark sincerity was tangible. "Listen, you got one over on me. Well played, baby. But we're entering new territory now. Are you sure you want to tease my cock like this?" He sat forward, letting his chest graze the tips of her breasts. His teeth tugged on her earlobe, making her shiver. "Because I won't be in these handcuffs forever. When I get out of them, I'm going to remember everything you do to me tonight."

Hayden swallowed. "Is that supposed to scare me?"

He scrutinized her face a moment. "Look at you. You're already scared. Afraid of a little pleasure, duchess? Worried you might actually like my middle-class mouth on you?"

She knew his intentions were to rile her up. Spark her temper. It worked. Once again, the need to prove he knew nothing about her rose to the surface. And maybe a tiny part of her recognized the accuracy of his words. Maybe she *was* afraid of pleasure. The kind of pleasure Brent might provide.

Her hands went to the hem of her skirt, drawing his attention away from her face. Very slowly, she slid the taut material up her thighs, revealing more and more of her black fishnet stockings. She watched as Brent shifted in front of her, hips tilting, chest shuddering. When she reached the point where her tights ended and she paused, he made a sound of protest. "Show me. You want to torture me? Fine. Just show me what's at the top of those fucking stockings."

Feeling a slight head rush over his fervent request, Hayden dragged the skirt higher and left it bunched around her hips. Apart from the rapid movements of his chest, Brent remained very still in front of her, his gaze fastened on the tops of her thighs where a crimson lace garter belt attached itself to her tights. She could see his arousal, thick and long, bulging against the zipper of his pants. She'd done that to him. Again, the heady rush of power made her bold. She stroked her hands down his chest, and circled her hips a little to show him what he couldn't have.

"I knew it." His gravelly voice startled her. "You walk around all day hiding fancy panties behind those expensive clothes, but you never let anyone have a taste of what's underneath." He ground his teeth together. "I think you're the one who needs to be taught a lesson."

"You think you know what I need?" She let her fingers brush over the tips of her breasts, smiling when he issued a strangled groan. "Enlighten me."

"Right now?" His gaze dropped once more to the material shielding her core. He gave a single, quick shake of his head. "You need a good tongue-fucking, duchess."

Breath whooshed from her lungs, and her legs began to shake. She'd never been spoken to in such a way and the rawness of it battered her senses. The ache between her thighs had turned insistent, demanding. All the energy, the nerves that had built up inside her needed release. *Now.* She looked at Brent to find him watching her, analyzing, holding his breath. Without waiting for her answer, he slid forward, nearly toppling her off the bench. Gasping, she braced her hands on the wall and lifted her hips to accommodate his body as it dropped to the floor. He came to rest with his head on the padded bench, and her thighs straddling his face—a position so erotic, her breath felt trapped in her throat.

"Slide your knees just a little wider, baby," he instructed. "Come and get your lesson."

What remained of her pride told her not to follow his arrogant command, but the painfully aroused part of her beat it back. She needed this. Involuntarily, her legs moved wider on the bench. When his mouth latched onto her, sucking her clitoris through the material, she cried out and grabbed the back of the bench for support. "Oh, God. *Oh, God.*"

"Lose the fucking panties and I can have you screaming those words."

She looked down, wondering how she could take her underwear off without standing and losing the drugging effect of his mouth. "H-how?"

"*Rip them*," he growled. "Believe me, if you hadn't cuffed me, I'd do it myself."

After a short pause wherein she wondered if she could do something so desperate, Hayden reached down and wrapped her fingers around the fragile silk. Then she ripped them off.

It felt amazing.

"Good girl."

She gripped the back of the bench tightly once more as Brent savored her in one, long lick. Then he returned to torture the pulsing bundle of nerves. He worried her clitoris between his lips, sucking gently, then tonguing the spot with tight, fast circles. On either side of his head, her thighs quivered so violently that the bench shook. She could feel a swift release coming, but didn't want the sensations to peak so soon. She wanted to savor. But when he sank his tongue deep inside her, searching her inner walls for that mysterious spot and finding it, finding it, *finding it*, she imploded. Fingers latched onto the bench, she writhed against his mouth as he wrung every ounce of pleasure from her trembling body.

"Brent! Oh my God, *Brent!*"

He turned his head and sank his teeth into her inner thigh. "Get the fuck down here, duchess. I need to be ridden."

She practically melted off the bench and onto his lap. Their mouths met in a wet, frantic kiss that made them both groan. Her fingers went to work unzipping his pants, taking a second to palm and squeeze his straining erection. His hips bucked into her hand, telling her how badly he needed his own release. She couldn't think beyond giving it to him.

Taking more for herself in the process.

"You have no idea what I'd do to you right now if my hands were free." He bit her bottom lip and tugged. "Right now, I'd be fingering your gorgeous pussy. Massaging that spot that got you to scream my name. Then I'd pick you up by your sweet little ass and sink you right down on top of me."

Her heartbeat pounded wildly in her ears, hands shaking as she finally freed his erection. He looked so incredibly full, smooth. Ripe. Hayden had the sudden, overwhelming urge to bring him to climax with her mouth.

When he saw her intention, his green eyes flashed urgently. "Fuck me with your mouth, baby. I'll do anything for it. Let me inside your sexy mouth."

She dipped her head, let it hover just above the tip of him.

And then the doorbell rang.

Chapter Three

Please. No, no, no. For the love of God, no.

Brent watched in stunned disbelief and utter horror as Hayden's rosy, well-kissed lips retreated from their position just above his cock and her head jerked toward the door. Awareness intruded on her features where there had been none just seconds before. *No, no, no*, his mind chanted on repeat.

He ached. Holy fuck, he ached. In a completely unexpected twist, the ice princess had turned out to be a blistering-hot sex goddess who'd barely even hesitated when he told her to rip off her own panties. She'd bested him at his own game, stripped for him, giving him a glimpse at the most insanely delicious body he'd ever had the pleasure of seeing up close. And then…*Christ*…the way she'd worked herself on his mouth…he would absolutely, 100 percent be storing that image for future use. He needed her to climb on and finish what they'd started. Didn't think he'd ever walk upright again until she did.

Please, if anyone up there is listening. If you make

whoever is on the other side of that door go away, I will give up watching baseball. Cheesesteaks. Fuck it. Beer. Anything. Just as long as she wraps those legs around my waist and finishes what we started.

"Hayden, look at me," he ordered, dragging her attention back to him. He lost his train of thought for a second when she turned to him, all swollen lips, messy hair, and passion-glazed eyes. She looked like a completely different girl from the one he'd walked in with. A fleeting thought swam through his mind. *This girl is twice as dangerous as smart-mouthed, uptight Hayden.* He shook his head quickly to clear it. "I don't give a good goddamn who is on the other side of that door. I'm in pain, woman. Fix it."

The hand still resting on his thigh tightened as if to soothe. She moved in toward him, gaze fixed on his mouth. *Yes, yes, yes. Please. Just a little closer.*

"*Hayden?*"

She froze. "Oh, freaking shitballs, it's my mother."

Handcuffed and with a hard-on to cut steel, Brent almost, *almost,* started to cry. Game, set, match. Nothing killed a woman's mood like her mother. His theory was proven two seconds later when Hayden stumbled to her feet and danced around as though looking for somewhere to hide him.

"Good luck finding somewhere to stuff my six-foot-five ass."

"Keep your voice down! And I can think of a *few* things I'd like to stuff in your ass." Wringing her hands, she shook her head. "That came out wrong. You know what I meant."

"Sure I do. You've got a fetish. I totally get it." He nodded toward the door and gave a quick chuckle to hide his arousal avalanche. After all, she was, for all intents and purposes, prancing around in front of him naked, no bra, no panties, skirt hiked up to her waist. *Kill me now.* "What's the play, duchess? You going to introduce me?"

Knock, knock. *"Hayden! Are you in there?"*

Tentatively, she walked toward the door, pulling her skirt back down to her knees as she went. Unmanly tears threatened once more as he watched her beautifully shaped ass disappear from view. *I'll never forget you, ass. Don't forget to write.*

"H-hey, Mom. I'm here."

A pause. "So then open the door, Hayden. I'm standing out here like a ninny."

"I, uh, can't open the door. I have the flu." She coughed. "I don't want to give it to you." Brent rolled his eyes and she flipped him the bird without even turning around.

"The flu! But we have that dinner party tomorrow night at Stuart Nevin's house. We told him weeks ago you'd be attending. He's looking forward to seeing you again."

Brent watched Hayden's posture deflate, her head drop forward against the door with a *thud*. Obviously she wasn't looking quite as forward to seeing this Stuart. Who was the guy, anyway? Probably some rich asshole with a bank account that could sink an oil tanker. He felt a flash of annoyance over having used even an ounce of brainpower to think about *Stuart*. Or whether or not he'd ever taken Hayden out on a date. Or whether *Stuart* had ever been treated to Hayden's Freaktastic Peep Show.

"I think it's just a twenty-four-hour bug." Cough. "I should be fine by tomorrow."

"Drink plenty of fluids and rest. I'll come by in the morning." A loud sigh. "I hope this isn't just another ploy to avoid the poor man, Hayden. He's very successful, you know. You're very lucky he's interested in you."

Brent's eyebrows rose at that backhanded insult, but Hayden couldn't see him. Her spine had stiffened, no doubt mortified over him overhearing this private conversation. He couldn't blame her. They tended to use every ounce of ammunition at their disposal against each other. She likely assumed this would be no exception. Then and there, Brent decided he wouldn't use this particular bit of ammo, ever. He didn't, however, intend to explore the *why* behind his decision. Only knew that it wouldn't feel honorable.

"Lucky. Huh." She smoothed a hand over her hair in a familiar gesture. Right in front of his eyes, he watched her transform back into the ice princess. Her back straightened, she tucked her hair neatly behind her ears and crossed her arms over her breasts. "See you in the morning, Mother. Sleep well."

"Good night, Hayden. No alcohol tonight. It makes your face puffy." Hayden didn't respond as Brent listened to the sound of her mother's heels clicking down the front steps. She snatched her bra off the ground in front of him and put it on, her motions jerky. Next came the shirt. *Bye-bye tatas.*

When she'd finished dressing, she pierced him with a look. "What? No comments from the peanut gallery? You've gone thirty seconds without shooting your mouth off. It's got to be some kind of record. Shall I call Guinness?"

Clearly, she needed a fight. Something to take her mind off the conversation with her mother. In his current state, he was all too happy to give it to her. "Maybe you should call a goddamn shrink, instead. You've got me handcuffed here with my family jewels hanging out, in case you somehow forgot. And you think you have any grounds to be pissed off? If I recall correctly, one of us had a screaming orgasm and it sure as shit wasn't me."

Her face reddened, probably matching his own. Her mother had upset her, then he'd finished the job by completely knocking the wind out her sails. Why he suddenly gave two shits about her mood, he couldn't decide.

He cleared his throat. "Listen, Hayden—"

She held up a finger to quiet him. "Hold on. I just had an

idea."

"Oh, really? Does it involve releasing me from unconstitutional imprisonment?"

"No." She pursed her lips. "What are you doing tomorrow night?"

"Why are you asking?"

"You like dinner parties?"

He threw his head back and laughed. "Me? Dressing up in a monkey suit and listening to your friends' amusing stories about their latest tropical vacation? Not going to happen, duchess."

Hayden shrugged off his rejection. "Fine. Thought you might relish the chance to crash one of the stuffy, overblown snooze-fests you're always teasing me about." She smoothed her skirt again. "I guess eating your weight in caviar and dropping backhanded insults on a bunch of rich stiffs doesn't appeal to you."

"Let's pretend for a moment that *did* appeal to me. What would be in it for you?"

"I get you as my bodyguard for the evening," she replied simply.

Brent's smile disappeared. Something unpleasant moved in his chest. "Why the hell would you need a bodyguard?"

Hayden waved off his serious tone. "I don't *need* one, per se. However, I'd like someone to keep Stuart away."

Brent could practically see the wheels spinning in her head, and braced for whatever would come next.

"If you happen to be your loud, irreverent self while we're there, thus pissing my mother off in the process? Well, I probably wouldn't mind that either."

"I see," he responded, berating himself for not anticipating the request. "You want to bring the working-class jackass from Queens along for your own personal amusement."

Her lips parted, she shook her head. "Wait—"

"Unlock the goddamn handcuffs. Now. The keys are in my pocket."

After a brief hesitation, she knelt down beside him. As she fished the keys from his pocket, their gazes met, but she quickly looked away. Having her close, her soft hand moving inside his pants, stiffened his cock once more, only serving to inflate his anger further.

She gasped when she saw that part of him stir, as though it should come as a surprise when he'd been primed for sex only minutes earlier. With the keys in her hand, she moved to unlock the handcuffs, then stopped. "When I take them off, you're not going to…I mean…"

"What? Throw you down on the floor and see if you fuck as hot as you kiss?" When she flinched a little, he reined himself in with a deep breath. "No. Even blue-collar jackasses have some boundaries. You're safe."

When his hands were finally free, he snatched the cuffs from her and carefully zipped his pants. He needed to get some air, clear his head. Which wouldn't be happening around her. As he yanked his shirt over his head, an idea of his own began to form. She expected him to show up to her ritzy party, acting like a knuckle-dragging ape? Hell, maybe he *would* put on a show. Just not the one she expected. Brent made sure the smile on his face stayed well hidden as he turned back to her, one hand on the doorknob.

"I don't have a suit. If you can get one in my size—and *good luck* with that, by the way—I'll go to your fancy dinner party tomorrow."

Her mouth fell open. "Wh-what?"

"Let me know. And Hayden?" He dangled her ripped panties in the air. "Later tonight, when I'm alone in my bed, stroking one out and thinking of the way you came like a freight train on my mouth, I'm going to make very good use of these."

Chapter Four

For the third time that afternoon, Hayden hung up before her call to Brent could be completed. She dropped onto her bed and buried her head in the plush goose-feather pillow.

"Stupid, overgrown, panty-stealing fucker," she groaned.

The situation last night had completely gotten away from her. One minute, she'd been totally in charge of the next move. She'd had Brent practically begging for anything she felt like giving him. And the next? Her very existence had seemed to depend on the whereabouts of his tongue. God, she hated him for making her feel so good. The damn nerve.

It had started as a game. To see who would cave first. Although now, if you asked her who had won, she would have no idea how to answer. He might have gotten the last word, but she'd gotten one singularly incredible orgasm during which she'd heard the faint strains of angels singing somewhere in the distance. She'd been so lost in what he was doing to her body, she'd almost made the colossal mistake of sleeping with him. On the floor in her entryway. With his hands cuffed behind his back.

When Hayden realized her breathing had become labored, she made a sound of disgust and pushed off the bed to pace toward the window. She looked out over the Hudson River and drummed her fingers against the pane of glass. Was she making a mistake? Seeing him again so soon after last night might be a terrible idea. Things had been so much easier when she looked at him and felt only intense loathing. If he came to the dinner party tonight, dressed in a suit, with a new, knowing look in his eye, she didn't feel 100 percent certain that would still be the case. Because while she still disliked him greatly...she wanted more.

Last night, when she'd been in the process of uncuffing Brent, she'd been a little disappointed when he *didn't* throw her down and have his dirty, pissed-off way with her. She'd been frustrated by her mother's visit, frustrated by the fact that she now felt a stunning sexual attraction for her nemesis...just flat-out frustrated. But he'd walked. She suspected because she'd bruised his ego, which actually, for once, hadn't been her intention. When the idea struck her to bring Brent along to the dinner party, she thought he'd jump at the chance to shock and mock her snooty family friends. Instead he'd seemed...hurt.

The reminder of the dinner party brought her to her next dilemma. After texting Brent for his suit size this morning, she'd made a few calls and found one that would fit his large frame. Mammoth-sized, to be exact. Now, when she should be calling him to arrange a time to drop it off, Hayden was balking. Did she really want to go down this road? First of all, showing up with an uninvited guest—a loud, filthy-joke-telling giant, no less—was considered a major faux pas in her world. Second, while she didn't mind the image of her scandalized mother, she would embarrass her father in the process. Now *that* bothered her.

Where her mother was stuffy and controlling, her father

had never been anything but warm and supportive. She would do anything for her father.

Well...the man she *called* her father, anyway. In reality, he'd never had a choice in the matter. When his younger brother's widow had shown up with their unwanted baby, he'd saddled himself with an adopted daughter, a young wife he barely knew, and a lifetime of responsibility. All to honor the memory of his brother.

Hayden sighed and glanced back at the suit laid out on her bed. She'd been debating about the wisest course of action since it was delivered half an hour ago. She could easily cancel and tell him no one in the city kept his size off the rack. But she had a feeling he'd sense her lie through the phone. Not to mention, she really didn't like the idea of Stuart Nevin and his grabby hands in her personal space all night. If Brent was good for one thing—okay, *two* things, because *damn*—it would have to be warding off unwanted male attention.

Decision made, she took a deep breath and hit redial on her cell phone. Brent answered on the third ring, classic rock music blaring in the background.

"Yeah?"

"Is that honestly how you answer the phone?"

A long pause. "Don't tell me you found a suit in my size."

Hayden let out the breath she'd been holding. "Unfortunately, yes. Someone passed on the number for a tailor who provides suits for the New York Rangers. And he *still* had to let out the shoulders a little bit."

"You didn't mind them last night when you were kneeling on them."

"Ten seconds." Her face flamed and she felt grateful he couldn't see her. "It took you ten seconds to make a crude joke about last night. Don't strain yourself trying to be original."

"That's what you want me for tonight, though, isn't it?" He snorted. "My ability to offend your people. I'm just getting warmed up."

Hayden frowned, once again confused by the tinge of hurt in his voice. She shook her head, certain she must be imagining it. "Are you working? Can I come drop it off at the precinct?"

"I'm not at the precinct," he said quickly. "It's my day off."

She held on to her patience when he didn't elaborate. "Okay. Are you home?" She checked her watch. "I can drive out to Queens. There shouldn't be much traffic this time of day."

"There is always traffic in this city." Brent scoffed. "Do you even know where Queens is? When's the last time you left Manhattan?"

No way would she tell him that she regularly left the borough to do work with her youth charity. She wouldn't do anything intentional to alter his horrible perception of her. It would imply that she cared what he thought, which she certainly did not. "Yes, I know where Queens is, you idiot. What's the address?" Hayden's brow wrinkled when she heard a loud, metal clang in the background and two men yelling.

"I'm, uh…" He cleared his throat. "Look, I'm helping out a friend today at his garage in Woodside."

"What do you mean? Like fixing cars and stuff?"

"Yeah, like fixing cars and stuff," he mocked. "And if you drive out here, I'll be more than happy to service you, baby."

As he laughed, she stomped toward her desk and grabbed a pen and paper. "Just give me the damn address before I change my mind."

After a short hesitation, he rattled off the address, then paused uncomfortably. "Listen, when you get here, call me. I'll come out to meet you. If you think my manners suck, you won't believe the things these guys will say if *you* walk in here."

She ignored the ridiculous flutter in her belly. "Why, Brent, I believe you just paid me some sort of awkward compliment."

"Not how I meant it. They'd probably whistle at just about anything on two legs."

"You are an enormous dick."

"Correction. I *have* an enormous—"

She hung up.

・・・

Brent checked his phone again, wondering what the hell was taking Hayden so long to get there. More than likely, she was tooling around this less-than-stellar neighborhood in her Mercedes without a care in the world. He still couldn't believe he'd given her the address to the garage. No one knew about his second job. Not even Daniel and Matt. She hadn't given him much of a choice, however, and now he'd have to deal with her condescension on top of everything else.

He rolled out from under a Cadillac and glanced toward the entrance. No luxury car in sight. He pushed to his feet and made for the bathroom, intending to clean some of the grease off before she showed. No reason to hand her any more insult material than she already had. When he flipped on the overhead light, he looked in the mirror and shook his head. She would have a field day seeing him like this, in stained coveralls and an ancient, backward Mets hat. He flipped on the water, watching as it filled the sink, but cut it off just as quickly.

Fuck this. He wasn't going to clean himself up for her. Putting on a fancy suit for tonight was one thing. After all, it would be worth it to see Hayden's reaction when he didn't require a lobster bib to keep it clean. But right now, he refused to hide the fact that he worked for a living. Had no reason to be ashamed of the fact that he got his hands dirty to support himself, his family.

His brother, Jordan, had just extended his tour overseas. The army only partially covered Brent's sister-in-law's expenses. They needed the extra money to keep both Brent's and Laurie's houses running while his brother was gone. His sister, Lucy, had a tuition payment coming due next week that his paycheck from the NYPD wouldn't completely cover. Then the mortgage. The list went on.

Brent heard a series of catcalls through the thin wooden door and cursed. She couldn't listen to him this one damn time, could she? He yanked open the door and stormed into the garage, the look on his face instantly silencing every vile thing being tossed in Hayden's direction. One by one, each mechanic promptly went back to work. They were smarter than he'd given them credit for. Finally, he turned to find Hayden standing at the entrance, her gaze fixed on him, mouth parted in a silent *O*.

He devoured her with a single glance, taking in black high heels, opaque stockings, and the short, *tight* gray dress she wore. He couldn't help it. Or look away. Couldn't stop his body's instant reaction. Last night, he'd been too busy slaking the unattended hunger she'd stirred up to think about the repercussions of their actions. Now he couldn't think of anything but getting her out of her clothes. Seeing her in those stockings. Was she wearing that garter belt again? Jesus, she'd made him hard from twenty yards away. If she knew how bad he wanted her, she would dangle herself in front of him like forbidden fruit every chance she got, just to torture him.

With one last warning glance at the other men, Brent closed the distance between them. He took her by the arm and pulled her toward the office located at the front of the garage. When they were inside, he slammed the door shut behind them and faced her.

"Well, good afternoon to you, too."

"I asked you to stay in your car."

"Since when do I follow orders from you?" She hung the gold-crested nylon garment bag she held on the back of the door. "Besides, I called you twice and it went to voice mail."

With a frown, he checked his pockets. Shit, he'd left his phone behind when he went to the bathroom. Still, he'd only been in there two minutes. "God forbid you be patient and wait. I know waiting for anything must be a foreign concept to a rich girl like you."

"Kind of like a shower is a foreign concept to you?"

"I work for a living, duchess," he said, taking a step closer, annoyed by the fact that she smelled so good, so expensive. "You should try it sometime."

Brent had the satisfaction of seeing her features cloud before she once again schooled them into a cool expression. She eyed the embroidered name patch on his jumpsuit. "I thought you were just helping out a friend. They just happened to have yeti-sized coveralls lying around with your name on them?"

"I help out a lot."

"Oh."

He could tell by her unconvinced tone that she didn't believe him. He'd been caught. Worse, she looked... concerned. Not exactly pitying him, just sympathizing over his need to work a second job. He didn't want it. Not from her. With a final step forward, Brent backed her into the desk. "You seem mighty interested in my work clothes. Thinking of the fastest way to get them off?"

When he grasped her hips and boosted her onto the desk, her breathing went shallow. "I didn't come down here to get pawed by your greasy mechanic hands."

"Why did you come down here?"

"To drop off your suit."

He leaned in and kissed the skin beneath her ear. "Is that what you told yourself, baby?"

"Don't call me that," she turned her head away, gave a halfhearted push against his chest. "What exactly are we doing here? We can barely tolerate each other. This is only going to make things more difficult."

"Is that enough to stop you?" He rested his hands on her legs and drew lazy circles with his thumbs on the inside of her thighs. When they inched just a little wider, he knew that she liked it. Feeling surprise when she didn't protest the touch of his dirty hands, he slipped his thumbs higher, just beneath the hem of her dress. "Would you like me to tell you what I did last night when I got home?"

"No." She shivered. "*Yes.*"

Brent chuckled quietly, but it came out sounding pained. "I took off my clothes and lay down on my stomach in bed. Then I wrapped your silk panties around my hand and fucked them."

When Hayden moaned and parted her legs further, he had to bite back the urge to yank her off the desk, turn her around, and push the skirt up over her ass. *Jesus. Where the hell am I taking this? Am I going to fuck her on a desk in a filthy garage? On a desk that isn't even mine?* It would definitely give the other mechanics something to catcall about, because if he let this encounter go on any further, she'd be moaning loud enough to shake the ceiling.

With a massive case of reluctance, he pushed her knees back together. When she started to voice a protest, he silenced her with his mouth, surprising them both. He gave in to the urge and parted her lips with his tongue, and took a brief but thorough taste. Slanted his mouth once, twice until he felt her melt. Then with a frustrated sigh, he pulled back.

When he saw her eyes were still closed, something lodged in his throat. Something he didn't like one bit. "Hey, rich girl. Wake up."

Her big brown eyes popped open and for one brief, intense second, he didn't have any choice but to kiss her again. Could think of nothing else but finding out if there was something more behind that dazed expression. Gently, he drew on her bottom lip, before giving the fuller top one the same treatment. When her eyelids fluttered, he melded their mouths together, surprised to hear the slow, contented noise issuing from both of their throats.

Brent was on the verge of deepening their contact when Hayden visibly shook herself and skirted past him toward the door, looking embarrassed at having let her guard down. For the second time in less than twenty-four hours, he watched her smooth her skirt back in place over her sexy little backside. His hands clenched at his sides to stop himself from reaching for her.

She ran a shaking hand over her slightly mussed hair. "So. W-we never discussed payment. What is this going to cost me?"

Had he just heard her correctly? "Excuse me?"

Even Hayden looked surprised at herself, but she quickly recovered. "I know your time isn't free. We're not friends. I don't expect any favors from you."

Brent wanted to be upset. A small part of him *definitely* resented the offer. Still, her flushed cheeks and downcast eyes told him that, while she never hesitated to insult him, this time she hadn't truly meant it as a put-down. He leaned back against the desk and crossed his arms. A wisecrack about taking sex as a form of payment hovered on the tip of his tongue, but he held back. If they ended up in bed together at some point—and right at this moment it seemed like a distinct possibility—he didn't want any confusion over why they'd ended up there. Either way, he had no intention of accepting money from her. "I don't know. What's the going rate for an escort nowadays? I hear they're all the rage with high-society girls." Hayden narrowed her eyes, but he held up his hand when she started to respond. "Why don't we just see how satisfied you are with my performance tonight? We'll decide then."

Hayden turned on a heel. "Dinner is at eight o'clock. I'll text you the address. Please don't be late." She pursed her lips. "On second thought, please be obnoxiously late and don't apologize. That ought to set the right tone."

"Oh, I'm going to set a tone. Don't worry."

"Fine," she responded with a healthy dose of suspicion. She turned to leave.

"Duchess?"

"Hmm?"

"You've got a little grease smudge on your nose."

The door slammed on his laughter.

Chapter Five

Hayden stood outside the luxury high-rise on Park Avenue, letting the September breeze cool her fevered skin. Sometime in the last hour, this little stunt she'd hatched with Brent had started to feel like a *really* bad idea. She checked her watch for the third time in under a minute, hoping he'd just blow her off and watch a baseball game or something instead. What had she been thinking? Brent, sipping wine and rubbing elbows with members of Manhattan high society? *She* could hardly manage it some nights. Brent would be like a bull in a china shop.

He probably thought he could waltz in, make a few jokes at their expense, and laugh his way back to Queens. What he didn't realize—what she *herself* had forgotten to take into account—was the fact that these people were vultures. They didn't let just anybody infiltrate their world. She'd been brought into it as an *infant* and she'd still never felt fully accepted. Now, Hayden was beginning to worry that she might be setting Brent up to be the butt of *their* jokes, instead of the reverse.

It shouldn't bother her. She shouldn't care one bit if he got a dose of his own medicine. But when she thought about Brent facing the firing squad also known as her parents' friends, she felt ill. She pulled her cell phone out of her pocket, intending to call him and cancel. Make a lame joke about rich people being so flighty. Tell him he'd been let off the hook, but she'd pay him anyway.

Pay him. She still couldn't believe she'd offered to do that. After he'd sufficiently scrambled her brain on that desk, kissing her in a way that made her ache, she'd sat there like an overinflated blow-up doll, mouth in round *O*. *O* as in *Oh, yes please. I'll take an* O *for the road*. For that moment, she'd forgotten who he was. Hell, she'd forgotten her own name. But nothing had prepared her for what came after, for the way he'd looked at her, let his mouth roam softly over hers as if he'd been…looking for something in her. She'd felt the pressing need to banish whatever she'd felt as he kissed her so reverently. So she'd blurted the first thing she could think of to redraw the battle line in the sand.

If she could go back in time and take back the offer of money, she would. Hayden didn't make a habit of wielding her privilege unnecessarily. Especially since it had never felt like *hers* to begin with. Then again, he hadn't exactly turned down the cash, had he? Hayden was pondering that confusing realization when she felt a warm hand curl around her elbow. She gasped and spun around to identify the hand's owner, dropping the phone in the process.

And landed hard against Brent.

"Whoa. Easy." He steadied her on her feet, then bent down to pick up her phone. "I know I'm tough to resist but save the fun stuff for later. We're in public, woman."

She glared up at him, still thrown off by his sudden appearance. "How about announcing yourself? You can't just go around grabbing women's arms on dark streets."

"I'm pretty damn easy to see coming if your face isn't buried in your phone."

"I was calling *you*."

"What for? I'm right on time."

"I see that." She bit her bottom lip, noticing for the first time how well he wore the suit. Never having seen him dressed in anything besides street clothes or his uniform, she had to admit he cleaned up well. Really well. His powerful chest and shoulders filled out the black jacket perfectly, the snug white shirt beneath tapering down into his matching dress pants. He looked every inch the gentleman. Too bad she knew better.

"See something you like?" His voice dropped low. "I'd be happy to skip this little shindig and let this suit spend the night on your bedroom floor."

"That's not happening." Her body's reaction didn't match her words, however. Toes curled inside her high heels, belly heated, skin prickled. "This thing between us ends now. In fact, I was calling you to cancel. I think avoiding each other for a while might be a good idea."

He came closer, backing her toward the building. "If you think you can get me into Manhattan on my day off in this fancy getup, then send me home before I've had a chance to make an impression, you're crazier than I thought. This is happening, duchess. I didn't shave twice in one day for nothing." The doorman held open the glass double doors as he walked her backward into the lobby and straight into an elevator. She looked at the doorman indignantly, but he merely cast an eye at Brent and shrugged as though to say, "As if I could stop him?"

When the elevator doors rolled shut, she reached over to punch the button for the twenty-third floor, but he caught her hand. "Let go of me."

Ignoring her command, he tugged her closer. Against

her will, she breathed in his fresh-from-the-shower scent. He braced his hands above her, trapping her against him and the wall. "Are you wearing that garter belt? Show me before we go in. I need a little motivation."

Hayden laughed in disbelief. "Motivation for what, exactly? I just told you that *this*"—she gestured back and forth between them—"isn't going to happen. Even you can agree it's a bad idea. If for no other reason, we need to knock it off for Daniel and Story's sake. It's bad enough we can't stand each other. If we add sex to the equation, it'll make things twice as messy."

"Our friends have nothing to do with this and you know it." He leaned in and sniffed—*sniffed!*—her neck. "Why don't you admit the real problem? You don't think you can make it through the night without jumping my bones."

When his tongue flicked out to taste the sensitive skin of her neck, she involuntarily tipped her head to the side to grant him access, which he immediately took advantage of, kissing and rubbing his lips over her damp flesh. "N-no. You can rest easy. I want no part of your bones. I'm just not so sure any more about embarrassing my parents."

Brent stilled his mouth's movements. "That embarrassment being me, right?"

"That's not—" Hayden cut herself off, reminding herself she didn't owe him apologies or explanations. "That's right. Color me shocked that you managed to show up looking halfway decent. I thought you might ditch the suit and show up in a bolo tie."

"I'd thought about wearing my Spider-Man costume, but it's at the cleaners."

With a snort, Hayden pulled away to search her phone for the private security code Stuart had texted her earlier, then punched it into the elevator's keypad. Brent stayed silent until the doors opened to reveal the foyer of Stuart's palatial penthouse, soft music and candlelight drifting toward them. Farther inside, she heard laughter and the clinking of glasses. The appetizing scent of a surely delicious dinner greeted them.

She would have rather been anywhere else at that moment.

Hayden started a little when Brent took her hand. He smiled tightly and led her out of the elevator. "Let the fireworks begin."

"Brent—"

"Hayden, is that you?" Her mother's voice rang out from the living room. "Dear, you're right on time to hear Stuart talk about his new investor for the com—" Her mother broke off as she and Brent rounded the corner, her eyes going wide as silver dollars. Hayden tried not to fidget as six other pairs of eyes, including her father's and Stuart's, landed on them. As always, her mother recovered quickly. "Well, well. Who is this?"

Drawing on years of practicing social niceties, Hayden smiled and drew Brent forward. She might feel like hurling, but no one else had to know. "Everyone, I'd like you to meet Brent. My date for this evening."

She watched her mother's nails dig into the white leather couch. Beside her, Brent let out a low whistle and she squeezed his hand to shut him up. "Date? You didn't mention you were bringing a date."

Hayden started to respond, but her father, who had been eyeing Brent speculatively, spoke up first. "Oh, uh, darling. This is all my fault. Hayden phoned me earlier at the office and told me." He turned to Stuart with a contrite look that deserved an award. "She asked me to call and let you know, but I got tied up on a conference call. My apologies. I trust there's room for one more?"

Stuart, who until now had been watching the proceedings

with poorly veiled disappointment, rose and started toward them. "Sure, why not? Hayden, you look beautiful as always," he said, kissing her cheek. When he lingered, Brent cleared his throat, drawing Stuart's attention. He held out his hand. "Stuart Nevin, nice to meet you."

Eyeing each other, they shook hands. "Brent Mason. Likewise."

If her stomach wasn't tied up in knots, Hayden might have laughed at the physical differences between the two men. Brent towered over Stuart, his giant hand all but swallowing the other man's smooth, elegant one as they shook longer than the introduction warranted. Stuart pulled back first, running his hand through his jet-black hair, looking less than thrilled.

Hayden's father stood to shake Brent's hand. "My daughter failed to mention she was bringing one of the Jets linebackers to dinner," he joked, with a wink in Hayden's direction. All at once, she felt horrible. She'd brought Brent with the intention of thwarting her mother's incessant matchmaking efforts, but any minute now Brent would say something intentionally offensive in front of her father. Whom she loved with all her heart. Who'd just covered for her, no questions asked.

Brent laughed. "With all their preseason injuries, the Jets need all the help they can get this year. Maybe I should take a chance and try out."

Her father brightened. "I take it you're into fantasy football?"

Brent confirmed with a nod. "Had my draft last week."

"Come sit," her father insisted, leading Brent away from her and toward the couch. "I need some advice on a trade. My office pool is so competitive..."

Hayden stood on the landing, watching in stupefied wonder as her father and Brent's discussion continued, growing more animated by the second. *What the hell just happened here?* The two other gentlemen, apart from Stuart, gathered around her father and Brent to join in their discussion. When they all laughed uproariously over something Brent said, Hayden turned to Stuart and asked him for a whiskey, neat.

By the time dinner was served, Brent had offered to dismiss everyone's parking tickets, told several riveting police stories to his now-captivated audience, and even performed the Heimlich maneuver on one of her father's associates, dislodging a green olive and earning the man's undying gratitude.

Hayden speared a perfectly cooked scallop with her fork when something Brent said made one of the older champagne-drunk socialites break out in high-pitched laughter.

As he launched into another story, he looked over and winked at her.

She'd been had.

• • •

"So I loaded him into the back of the squad car and told him, 'Next time, bring ski boots.'"

Around him, the men dissolved into laughter and Brent tossed back the remains of the girly drink he'd been handed after dinner. Storytelling could be thirsty work. Especially when you could practically feel daggers being stared into the back of your head by a certain someone in sexy stockings.

"So how does one become an explosives expert?" Hayden's father asked, leaning back in an antique chair that cost more than Brent's mortgage. "It seems like a dangerous choice, running toward the bomb when everyone else is running the opposite direction."

"It definitely requires a certain level of insanity. In fact, I'm pretty sure that's listed in the job description." Brent shrugged. "At least there aren't people lined up to replace me."

"I'd imagine not," Stuart commented absently as he sipped a glass of wine.

Amused, Brent let a beat pass before filling the silence. "I was lucky. My father was a cop, too. He recognized that I had a knack for it. Most parents get upset when you blow up your sister's Barbie Dreamhouse. My father took me to an explosives demonstration instead."

The older woman he'd been mentally referring to as Socialite Number Two laughed. "Is your father...*tall* like you?"

Grr-owl. One ticket to Cougartown, please. Brent glanced in Hayden's direction, swallowing a laugh when she tossed back most of her drink. "Nope. Got the height from my mother. My parents met for the first time at a bar." He leaned forward as if imparting a secret. "When the bartender asked my father for his drink of choice, he infamously responded, 'Nothing for me. I've already got a tall drink of water right here.'"

Hayden burst out laughing, but quickly reined it in when she seemed to realize all eyes were trained on her. "Um. Where is your father now?"

"Retired in Florida. Last time I went for a visit, he was rebuilding the engine on a sixty-eight Pontiac Firebird in the driveway. Mom calls it his playtime."

Stuart raised a lazy eyebrow. "You know cars?"

Brent watched as Hayden's drink paused halfway to her mouth. She was obviously petrified of him revealing his second profession, embarrassing her in the process. Reminding himself he didn't give a damn what anyone else thought, Brent cleared his throat, keeping his eyes squarely on Hayden. "Yes. Actually, I moonlight as a mechanic."

Two seats away, her mother's fork scraped along the

expensive china. Stuart, however, couldn't have looked more pleased. "One of my Aston Martins needs a new alternator." He propped his ankle on his knee, smiling smugly at Brent. "Can I trust you with it?"

Brent saluted him with his drink, ignoring the pang in his chest when Hayden rose quickly and left the room. "You can trust me to overcharge you."

Stuart smiled on cue, but it didn't reach his eyes. Brent forced himself to remain seated when the man got up a moment later and followed Hayden from the room. Just as he made the decision to go after them, Hayden's father threw another question his way, but he could barely focus on it.

Last night, when he'd been handcuffed and blue-balled within an inch of his life in Hayden's foyer, he'd let her think he was going to show up and act like the big clown she perceived him to be. Instead, he'd prove to her that she didn't have the first clue about him or what he was capable of. That using the right fork and shooting the shit with millionaires was a breeze when compared with dismantling a pipe bomb or rescuing injured civilians from a structural collapse.

And maybe, just a small part of him had wanted to prove it to himself. He didn't lack familial affection in his life. His parents, his sister and brother, his nieces...they were all grateful for the work he put in to keep their lives running smoothly and they never hesitated to tell him. They depended on him and he loved that. It drove him. But sometimes he wondered if he spent so much time making ends meet, he was forgetting himself. Defining himself by how much money he made per week. How many problems he could solve with each paycheck. It may have been unconscious, this need to prove he could accomplish something that didn't involve a wrench or C4, but he couldn't deny an odd satisfaction at having fit in tonight, without sacrificing his identity in the process.

He hadn't forgotten his other reason for being there

tonight, though. After Stuart spent the entire dinner with his eyes glued to Hayden's breasts, Brent's teeth were still on edge, even as he strove for casual. Not that he could fault the guy. The girl might be spoiled and thoroughly exasperating, but she had an amazing rack. He'd sneaked in more than a few peeks himself. Stuart, however, had all but danced on the table pointing at them, shouting "Gimme, gimme, gimme!"

Stuart. Damn, even the guy's name annoyed the shit out of him. He shouldn't care if the two snobs ended up together. Hell, they deserved each other. But he couldn't deny feeling a whole heap of aggravation over the idea. It had to be the lust talking. She'd left him unsatisfied last night and until he had her, apparently this territorial feeling would eat him alive. If he had his way, it wouldn't be much longer. Whether or not they could stand to share the same air, he wanted her like hell.

Brent scratched the back of his neck, feeling anxious. He didn't like Hayden and Stuart being outside his line of vision. She didn't want to be alone with him. It had been one of the reasons she'd brought him along.

Trying to tamp down the twitch of alarm, Brent set down his glass on a crystal coaster and rose from the couch, murmuring an excuse as he went. She hadn't mentioned *why* she wanted Stuart kept away, had she? Brent's stride increased in pace. He'd just turned down the hallway leading to the kitchen when he heard voices.

"Come on, Hayden. You know you just brought him here to make me jealous. It worked. Is that what you want to hear?"

She sighed. "Actually, I couldn't care less." Her heels clicked then stopped short. "Stuart, I need to get back to my mother. Move out of the way. You've clearly had a lot to drink."

"A cop, though? Honestly, sweetheart."

Hayden said something Brent couldn't hear.

"Fine, then. Why don't we try to make him a little jealous instead?"

"*No.*"

Brent had heard more than enough. His vision swam a little as he entered the kitchen and saw Hayden wedged between Stuart and the marble island, clearly trying to ward him off. He dug his fingers into his palms and breathed deeply through his nose. Hayden's eyes shot wide when she saw him, alerting him to the fact that his temper was showing on his face. Stuart followed her line of vision, backing off immediately when he saw Brent. It took every ounce of willpower he had inside him not to grab Stuart by the neck and toss him like a rag doll across the room. But a small voice of reason told him he'd come this far in proving to her he wasn't some hotheaded idiot. He couldn't blow it now.

Brent nodded once at Stuart. "You're wanted in the living room."

"Very well." He looked at Hayden. "Are you coming?"

"No, she's staying," Brent responded before he could stop himself. Her posture stiffened slightly at his high-handedness, but he couldn't summon the will to care. Currently, his will was all tied up. After a moment of tense silence, Stuart shrugged and proceeded to leave the kitchen, cocktail in hand. Brent stopped him with a hand on his arm before he could pass, then leaned in and spoke quietly so Hayden wouldn't overhear.

"If you have trouble understanding the word 'no,' I'll be more than happy to explain what it means. Especially when she says it."

Stuart stiffened, but continued walking after a moment without looking back.

"Well? You've ordered me to sit and stay, master. Now what?"

Brent didn't answer, just rounded the island in her direction with long strides.

"Don't you need to get back to your pack of admirers? They're bound to miss their new dude crush." When he didn't answer again, she frowned. "Why are you looking at me like that? It's not as though I encouraged him. I came in here for ice and he followed me. Not that it's any of your business."

Brent stopped in front of Hayden, forcing her to tilt her head back. "Yes, it is. You told me you wanted him kept away. It's part of the reason you brought me here."

She shook off his words. "I can handle Stuart without your help. Besides, you were a little busy playing *teach the rich girl a lesson* to notice anything else."

"You're right. I'm sorry."

"Listen—" She did a double take. "You're *what?*"

He smiled. "I'm sorry. If you'd told me in advance how bad he was, I wouldn't have let him within ten feet of you. We have our differences, Hayden, but I'd never let some asshole put his hands on you if I could prevent it. I have a sister. A mother. I take that kind of thing seriously."

"Oh." She stared up at him like he'd sprouted antennae. "*Oh.*"

His lips twitched. "Oh?"

Then in a move he didn't see coming, Hayden dug her fingers into his hair and pulled him down for a hot, hard, whiskey-flavored kiss. What little willpower Brent still possessed flew out the window when her tempting curves molded to his and she sucked on his tongue with a throaty moan. He sucked her tongue right back, letting his hands drop to her ass and knead the taut flesh beneath her skirt. It felt natural, inevitable, to lift her against him so she could wrap her legs around his waist, fitting their lower bodies together with a perfection that made him groan roughly into her mouth. Once he had her resting on top of his erection, he gripped her ass and slid her up and down, so she could experience every inch of it against her core.

"Baby, I'm going to fuck you tonight. You know that, don't you?"

"Yes," she whispered against his mouth. "But I need s-something right *now*, okay?"

He backed her into the counter, grinding himself into her soft, inviting center. It felt like heaven and hell at the same time. His body demanded release. Now. *Now.*

Just a while longer, the sane part of his brain chanted. They weren't alone yet. He couldn't have her here. God, did the freaking universe hate him lately? "What do you need, duchess? We need to hurry."

Maintaining their hot eye contact, she unhooked her legs from around his waist and slid down him, slowly enough to short-circuit his brain. Taking his hand, she shocked him once again by guiding it underneath her skirt to the silk between her legs. "Make me come, Brent."

"Fuck," he ground out, quickly pushing the silk aside. His cock ached, his tongue had gone fuzzy, and all he could think about, *care* about, in that moment was bringing the girl in front of him to an earth-shattering climax. She'd made the request as though her life depended on him giving her pleasure. It made him want to beat his chest with his fists, proving to her once and for all what a caveman he was.

When his fingers touched her naked flesh for the first time, the smooth, slick heat almost robbed him completely of rational thought. He knew she wanted his fingers to massage her clit but nothing could prevent him from sinking his middle finger deep inside her, giving it a quick upward thrust. Her inner walls contracted, milking his finger so tightly, he could barely draw it out.

"More, Brent," she whimpered softly. "Again."

"Don't worry." He granted her two more quick thrusts,

then moved his wet fingers to the tight bundle of nerves, pressing tight and holding. "You're going to be full of me later. For now, just let me rub your sweet little clit."

On a raspy breath, she parted her lips to receive his hot, openmouthed kiss while his fingers worked between her legs. He savored each sob of pleasure he wrung from her on his tongue. Her hips shook and swiveled until he was forced to hold her completely still against the counter with his body so he could finish her. In the back of his mind, he heard the voices in the living room grow louder. Closer?

When he felt her begin to pulsate and tighten, he increased the circular motion of his fingers. "Come on, baby. We're out of time." Dammit, the footsteps were growing louder. He leaned forward and spoke right against her ear. "Come for me *right now* and I'll let you ride me as hard as you want later. I know what gets you off. I saw it in your eyes last night. You want to throw me down and fuck me, duchess? Good. I'm in the mood to let you."

At the last second, he swooped down and caught her moan with his mouth while she shook, savoring her dampness on his fingers. He heard footsteps coming down the hallway the same time she did. As fast as humanly possible, they pulled her skirt into place and he hid his tented lap behind the marble island.

One of the older ladies swayed into the kitchen, a little unsteady on her feet from too much wine. She stopped short when she found them already occupying the kitchen, then gave Brent a knowing look.

"Were you stealing a kiss in here, mister?"

Brent held up his hands. "You caught me."

Behind him, Hayden slumped against the counter.

Chapter Six

After paying the driver, Brent exited the cab and opened the door for Hayden. Standing above her, silhouetted by the streetlight, he looked larger than life holding out his hand. Waiting for her to take it. She hesitated a moment, suddenly unsure of her decision to bring him home. Admittedly, she wanted him. Badly. At some point, however, it had started feeling like more than just a passing attraction. Somehow, Brent, the person she'd always thought understood her the least, seemed to know exactly what she needed. She herself hadn't known until he'd said the words in Stuart's kitchen. Words that now echoed in her head, heating her blood, making her skin tingle. *You want to throw me down and fuck me, duchess?* Yes, yes, yes. That's exactly what she wanted.

"You going to stay in there all night?"

Rolling her eyes to hide her jumbled emotions, she took his hand and let him lead her up the stoop to her front door. Once they reached the top, she busied herself trying to find her keys in her purse, but his big hand closed over hers, ceasing her jerky movements. "Hey. I want you, duchess. Bad as hell. But if you're not completely here with me, I'll go."

"You would, wouldn't you?" She peered up at him, wondering if this other dimension to him had always existed and how she'd missed it. *I have a sister. A mother. I take that type of thing seriously.* She'd never thought of him as anything but a vulgar meathead. Was it possible she'd been wrong? "What else don't I know about you, Brent?"

Watching her closely in that distracting way of his, he didn't answer. Then, in a replay of the previous night, Brent followed Hayden into her town house and pushed her up against the heavy front door. They regarded each other warily as bodies pressed together, hands roamed over curves, breathing harshened.

Hayden felt as though her body would combust at any second. She wanted him with a single-mindedness that alarmed her and didn't give a damn about the consequences or the fact that they were supposed to hate each other. Or whether or not tomorrow she would wake up and regret sharing her body with someone who usually regarded her with contempt. How did this infuriating man manage to make her feel so incredibly sexy and uninhibited? Never before, not once, had a man gotten this reaction out of her. This relentless need to get and give pleasure. She felt weak and strong at the same time. Unsure, yet determined.

In the back of her mind, however, a little voice whispered that she needed to keep a leash on this crazy attraction running wild between them. The unfamiliar frightened the hell out of her, especially when so many uncertainties lay between herself and Brent. For all she knew, he wanted to take her to bed so he could use it against her. From this night forward, every time she leveled an insult in his direction, he wouldn't have to utter a single word in response. The memory alone of her begging him to make her come would be enough to keep her quiet.

Another part of her wasn't so certain he would use their physical relationship against her. He'd managed to surprise her twice tonight. First, by winning over her parents' tight-knit group of friends, then again when he apologized for letting Stuart near her. She couldn't yet allow herself to consider that Brent had been a classy gentleman all this time hiding underneath a Mets baseball cap, but...perhaps there was more than met the eye.

It was too soon to take that chance. This other Brent, the one she'd briefly glimpsed under the surface, might be a figment of her imagination. Someone she'd conjured up to justify the insistent desire he'd generated in her. With all these doubts swirling in her head, Hayden put a hand on his big chest and held him back. They would satisfy this inconvenient craving tonight, but dammit, there needed to be some ground rules.

"This is a one-time thing, right?" Hayden asked, wetting her lips. "For some odd reason, we seem to want each other, so let's get it out of our systems. Then we move on. Agreed?"

His hands coasted down over her breasts, groaning when he encountered her stiff nipples. "Woman, if it means getting your clothes off, I'd agree to change my name to Florence right now."

Hayden laughed before she could stop herself, marking the first time she'd ever laughed at one of his jokes. They both paused, acknowledging that fact with their eyes, before his hands resumed their exploration of her body. His mouth claimed hers in a heated kiss as he unzipped her dress, then tugged it over her shoulders and down her hips. His tongue stroked in and out, seeking, teasing.

After a moment, she tore her lips away. "We don't speak about tonight, either. Ever again. None of our friends find out. And no jokes about it, Brent. Promise."

"Florence, Hayden. Florence."

She ducked her head so Brent wouldn't see her smile, but he was too busy watching her dress fall to the floor, revealing her black lace bra-and-panty set, complete with garter belt and stockings. Her tummy flipped a little when he cursed under his breath and ran a hand over his open mouth. His hot regard felt heavy as it ran the length of her body, pausing at her thighs and between her legs.

He tucked one finger into the top of her stocking, sliding it back and forth slowly. Hayden felt each movement between her legs as though he were touching her there instead. She grew increasingly damp with each drag of his finger. "I hate these stockings. Don't ever stop wearing them."

Hayden sucked in a breath as his finger slipped around to the back of her thigh. "I-I don't understand. That makes no sense."

His hand traveled higher to cup her behind, fitting her against him. "Every time you cross your legs, I hear that material rub together." He ran his tongue and teeth down the side of her neck. "Your tight thighs, covered in silk, parting and crossing. Parting and crossing. Only you never leave them open long enough for me to see your pussy. It makes me crazy."

She writhed against the door, his provocative words ratcheting her need even higher. "What are you waiting for? An apology?"

"I have a much better idea." He grasped her around the waist and deposited her on the bench. The same bench they'd used the night before. She watched, dumbfounded, as he knelt down in front of her, gaze fastened on the juncture of her thighs. "Show me right now. Cross and uncross your legs for me, duchess. I want to see how it looks when there's no skirt to hide behind."

Hayden's chest felt tight, her skin enflamed. Every nerve ending in her body hummed with dizzying arousal. She obeyed his order simply to witness his reaction. Could do nothing else. The first time she crossed her legs, then slowly parted them, she felt his loud growl of approval deep in her belly, vibrating and heating. The second time she let her stocking-clad thighs cross and uncross, he unzipped his pants and reached inside to stroke himself as he watched her, eyes dark with lust.

"Very good. Lose the bra and do it again."

Trying to keep her breathing steady and failing, Hayden unhooked the clasp between her breasts and let the material fall down her arms. Once again, that low, almost-angry sound emanated from his throat. This time, she moaned in response, letting her head fall back on her shoulders. Of their own volition, her hands rose to palm her breasts, thumbs caressing her peaked nipples. Her body felt hot, shaky. His riveted gaze felt like a touch in itself, moving across her skin, memorizing, devouring.

Brent's arm banded around her waist, startling her, so lost she'd been in her own pleasure. He picked her up off the bench and rose. She wrapped her legs around his waist, mouth immediately seeking his for a hot, desperate kiss. One of his hands sank into her hair, angling her head. The other kneaded the flesh of her bottom.

"Bedroom. Where is it?" he grated against her mouth. "I need to fuck you."

She nodded toward the back of the town house, and Brent's long strides ate up the distance between the semi-dark living room and her bedroom. Halfway there, she forgot to direct him and began nipping and licking his neck until Brent was forced to push her up against the hallway wall outside her bedroom and punish her mouth for distracting him. Finally, he stumbled them into her room, letting her slide down his body at the foot of the bed.

He maintained intense eye contact with her as he quickly

stripped out of his suit. When Hayden started to roll the tights down her leg, he stopped her with a harsh sound. "Don't you dare take them off." His pants and belt hit the floor. "You never want to discuss what happens here tonight? Fine. But I'm going to remember what it's like to be between all that silk. There's nothing you can do to make me forget." He came toward her slowly, stalking her. "I'm going to think about it. Often. While you're lying here at night in your big, comfortable bed, I'll be remembering. Over and over."

Hayden refused to back up even a step as he reached her, his expression fierce. "I can't control what you choose to think about," she responded with more bravery than she felt.

Perusing her body, he shook his head. "No. You sure as hell can't." His big hands settled on her hips, flexed. "You've got control right now, though. Take it. Before I take it from you."

Inside her, apprehension mixed with excitement, so heady her hands shook. *This is what you wanted*, Hayden reminded herself. She'd been struggling to find the missing piece for so long. This could be it. He'd put her in charge. Why was she hesitating? Part of her nerves sprang from the unknown. How deep did the need run? Why had it taken an enemy's touch to make her realize it?

"Hayden..." he rasped, fingers digging into her flesh.

Now or never. Hayden brought her hands to his shoulders and pushed him with all her might onto the bed. He landed on his back, head coming up immediately to watch her next move. She moved over him on hands and knees, reveling in the way his chest rose and fell rapidly, his erection lying thick and ready on his ridged belly. She took a moment to appreciate the sheer maleness of him. His size, the texture of his skin, his muscular build. Once more, her eyes were drawn to the hard length demanding her attention. After the briefest hesitation, she skimmed her fingers down his belly and wrapped him in her fist. His hands dug into the comforter as his hips bucked.

"Put it in your mouth. *Now*, baby." He spoke through clenched teeth. "I've been waiting for it since last night. Nothing I do makes it better. It needs to be your mouth."

Very slowly, she licked the tip, power curling in her belly when he hissed through his teeth. She did it again, this time letting her tongue linger until his hips lifted impatiently. Then she took all of him in her mouth, as deep as she could, sucking hard all the way back to the tip as Brent shouted obscenities at the ceiling. "Is that what you wanted?" she purred against the smooth skin.

"*Fuck yes.*" He twisted the comforter in his fists. "*More.*"

"More of this?" Watching him innocently, she ran her tongue around the head in circles. "Or this?" She closed her mouth around him and took him to the back of her throat, sucking once again until she reached the head. Then she flicked her tongue against him with tiny, teasing licks.

He threaded his fingers roughly into her hair, bringing her head up to meet his tortured gaze. "I've tongued and fingered you, now it's my turn. Give me what I need, baby. I'm dying."

"When I'm ready. *Baby.*" Without thinking about her actions, simply obeying what felt right, she pinned his wrists against the bed and scraped her teeth over his belly, biting and licking the fevered skin as it shuddered under her mouth. When she took him back between her lips and finally gave him what he needed, she refused to stop stroking him with her mouth until his voice grew strangled from begging her to end the torture.

Hayden reached into her bedside drawer and handed him a condom. As he rolled it down his length, she played with her nipples, tempting him to hurry. She straddled him, her knees pressing into the mattress on either side of his hips.

He gripped himself in his big hand and sought her entrance, rubbing the plump head back and forth through her damp center.

"No more games." Brent thrust into her halfway. "Ride me hard or not at all."

Hayden wiggled her hips, stretching as she took more of him inside her. He gave an upward thrust, pushing deeper and deeper until she whimpered.

"Jesus, baby." He groaned loudly, shifted. "Been a while?"

Yes. "No. It's just you…you're…"

Brent sat up, putting his face right in front of hers. He bit her bottom lip and tugged. "I'm what?" When she tried to kiss him, he dodged her mouth. "Say it. What am I?"

"Huge," she whispered.

"That's right." His hands slipped up her back and gripped her shoulders. "And you're going to take it."

He pulled down on her shoulders, while at the same time driving his hips upward, imbedding himself deep inside her. Hayden's head fell back and she screamed.

"Fuck, fuck, *fuck*," Brent chanted gruffly against her ear. "Oh God, Hayden, you've got such a snug little pussy."

She felt impaled. Full. As though if she moved, her entire body would shatter into a thousand pieces. Already her thighs and stomach had begun to tremble. Brent gave her one hard kiss, then lay back down as if handing her the reins. His hands shook as they stroked up and down her thighs, telling her how much it cost him to give her control.

Wanting to please him as much as she needed to assuage the ache building within her, Hayden moved her hips once, testing, and nearly sobbed at the tingling heat that shot through her system, concentrated between her thighs. Brent's eyes were squeezed shut, fingers digging into her skin as he muttered a curse. She braced her hands on his shoulders and increased her pace, angling her hips so she could rub against Brent where she needed him most. Sensations slammed through her with each roll of her hips, so intense, so foreign that she had to slow her movements to let her mind catch up with her body.

"Hayden. Look at me," Brent growled beneath her. "Move those hips faster, or I'll put you on your back. Do you understand?" Then his hand reared back and slapped her ass. Hard.

"Ah!" A struggle took place inside of her. She couldn't deny the exhilaration that rushed through her as his hand connected with her skin. Possibly even wanted him to do it again. Yet at the same time, she wanted to berate him for touching her that way. For confusing her already-haywire emotions. "I'm going to kill you," she whispered.

He sat up once more, wrapped her hair around his fist and growled. "Fuck me, instead."

Something dark and dizzying raced through her. Need for pleasure. Need to wipe the arrogance off his face. Pure *need*. She pushed him back down onto the mattress and rode him with fast, bucking movements of her hips. Brent threw his head back on the pillows, face twisted into an expression of intense pleasure/pain, encouraging her further. She took his hands and leaned back, altering the angle without slowing her pace, and they moaned simultaneously at the new friction.

"That's perfect, baby. Feel how deep I am?"

The beginning of her climax sizzled through her. She felt it coming, raced toward it, her body undulating atop him. Faster, faster, until she felt it scream across her nerve endings, tugging and exploding through her system like nothing she'd ever experienced.

"Brent! Oh my God."

"Hang on, duchess. This isn't over." As the orgasm continued to wreak havoc on her senses, she felt Brent flip her over onto her back. He hooked his arms under her knees, drew them high and wide. Before she could guess his intentions, he began pounding into her, his thrusts deep and powerful. Hayden reveled in each one, each grunt of pleasure against her neck as he worked for his own release. She'd made him lose his control, turned him into an animal. It thrilled her.

As the promise of another orgasm tightened her middle, she dug her nails into his shoulders and raked them down his back, loving it when he bit her neck and pumped his hips faster. "Harder, Brent. Even harder."

With a snarl, he wrenched her knees higher. "You think you can handle harder?"

"Can you give it?" she countered.

Keeping his gaze locked on hers, he drove into her with such force, the headboard of her bed slammed against the wall. Her insides quaked with the oncoming climax. Lost to the searing heat, Hayden gave in to an urge. Couldn't stop herself. She raised the hand digging into his back and brought her palm down on his ass with a loud slap that echoed through the room. And watched him come apart.

"Oh, sweet Jesus, Hayden." He threw his head back, eyes closed on a groan. "I have to come now, baby. It's too fucking good." His movements changed, grew staggered. Seeing his reaction, his loss of control, pushed Hayden over the edge once more and they moaned as they found their peak together.

Chapter Seven

Brent lay on his back in Hayden's bed, still trying to catch his breath. He let his eyes wander over her bedroom for the first time as he racked his brain for something to say, something to explain what had just taken place between them. Since entering the room, he'd seen nothing but her. Decorated simpler than he would have imagined, the interior looked plush and rich nonetheless. Three floor-to-ceiling windows lined the west wall, looking out over the Hudson River. A billowy white canopy he'd neglected to notice draped down from the ceiling, resembling clouds over the bed.

He glanced over at Hayden where she sucked in deep breaths, her beautiful body slick with perspiration beside him, then quickly averted his eyes. The girl next to him, the girl who'd ridden him like the sexiest damn cowgirl he'd ever seen, looked nothing like the Hayden he'd come to know. Hair in a tangle, cheeks flushed with exertion, eyes clouded with wanting him…she'd been his secret fantasy come to life.

But that's all she wanted him to be. A secret. His eyes landed on a chaise longue in the corner. He could just see her draped across it, pearls around her neck, diamonds in her ears. Laughing as she talked to some wealthy asshole on the phone. She belonged to a very different world. One he had no desire to be a permanent part of. One she had no desire to include him in. He needed to remember that. When he looked at her again, he needed to remember that tomorrow she would go back to being made of ice and this night would live on only in his memory. When he walked out the front door, he'd never see *this* girl again. He'd only see Hayden Winstead, smug, sophisticated heiress.

His first instinct was to make a joke. Put them back in that place they'd grown comfortable with. Two people who could barely tolerate each other. But he stopped himself. She would expect that of him. Tomorrow would be soon enough for things to return to normal.

Normal. He almost laughed. Now that he knew what lay underneath her carefully polished surface, he'd have one hell of a time pretending. A sexually frustrated bad girl dying to be let out. He'd managed to glimpse it, encourage it even. If he allowed himself to consider the possibilities of what she could use him to discover about herself, he would never leave, so he demanded that his brain stop thinking about it. About her sliding up and down his cock, how it felt inside her...how she'd spanked him. How he'd kind of *loved* it.

No. Don't even think about it. She wanted a one-time thing. He'd be damned before he suggested anything different. No way in hell would he open himself up for her condescending ridicule when he wanted more than she did. The girl beside him was merely an illusion. Even if she came alive in bed, under his touch, he knew her true identity. Spoiled, rigid, and most importantly, from a different world. This is where they started and ended.

A memory of her face softening in Stuart's kitchen, just before she kissed him, drifted through his consciousness, followed by an image of how she'd looked laughing at his joke earlier. Eyes bright, lips tilted in amusement. *No. Not real. Not real.*

Banishing the memories, Brent blew out a breath and laughed with more humor than he felt. "I guess it's a good thing we promised never to talk about tonight. If the guys knew I let a girl spank me, I'd never hear the *rear* end of it. Pun intended."

Hayden giggled. For some reason the sound made his throat feel tight. "You'd be the butt of their jokes for weeks. Pun also intended."

"Yeah. That's at the *bottom* of my list."

She nodded on the pillow. "No, I get it. You draw the liney at your hiney."

Their shared laughter mingled in the dark room, confusing Brent further. This Hayden, the one making dorky-sweet puns that called to his inner goofball, was beginning to feel real to him and he couldn't allow that to happen. Tonight couldn't lead anywhere. Even if there were more layers to her he hadn't been aware of, he didn't belong in her fancy town house any more than she belonged in a greasy car garage, or a dirty downtown precinct. Naked and boneless, nestled among gazillion-thread-count sheets, she looked mouthwatering. When he felt himself begin to harden again, readying for more of the best sex he'd ever experienced, Brent knew he had to get out of there.

Hayden seemed to become aware of their unusual position at the same time he did. Lying together in the moonlight, trying to make each other laugh. Most importantly, not fighting. The easy, languid smile vanished from her face and she stiffened, gaze skittering away.

When she tugged the sheet higher over her breasts, Brent sat up and threw his legs over the side of the bed. Unconcerned about his nakedness, he rounded the bed and pulled on his pants. "When do I need to return this suit? I'd leave it with you now, but I don't think the city would let me keep my job if I rode the subway home stark naked."

"Oh, um, right..." Hayden sat up and tucked her dark, unruly hair behind her ears. She looked so fragile in the center of the enormous bed, so uncharacteristically unsure all of a sudden, that he hated himself for getting up so abruptly. He fought the urge to toss the pants back on the ground and join her again. Coax the confident sex kitten back to the surface. "The tailor's card is in the inside pocket. It's a two-week rental, so there's no rush."

Brent acknowledged that with a nod and continued dressing, painfully aware of the awkward silence in the room. Also positive that if she gave him the slightest encouragement, he'd be back between the sheets with her in seconds.

"Brent?"

He froze in the act of buttoning his shirt. "Yes?"

"What did you say to Stuart earlier? In the kitchen, I mean."

Disappointment settled thick his gut. "I asked him if he needed an explanation of the word 'no.' That's all."

She stared at him in silence for a moment. "Thank you."

When their gazes locked across the bed, he didn't think he could walk out the door. It felt like sacrilege, leaving her behind looking mussed-up and vulnerable. She wanted one night only? Hell, it wasn't even midnight. Didn't they at least have until morning before reverting back to their old ways?

"Hayden..." He trailed off. Asking for more would be a big step. She could very well say no. Was it worth the risk? *God, yes.* "Listen, I, uh—"

"Oh!" She visibly shook herself, her face transforming with...embarrassment? A robe went on over her shoulders as she crossed the room. Brent watched in confusion as she picked up her purse and removed a wallet. "We never discussed…what you wanted to be paid for tonight. Just tell me how much you wanted…whatever you think is fair." Finished with her ramble, she looked up at him expectantly.

It took Brent a moment to process her meaning. When it finally hit him, anger washed over him in a wave. Here he stood, about to beg for another few hours in her bed, when she'd merely considered him a business transaction. He averted his eyes. "You certainly didn't waste any time putting me in my place, duchess."

She paled, the purse dropping to her side. "I thought…"

"You thought what? I'm so hard up for cash that I need to suffer through three hours of canapés and smooth jazz to make a buck? Keep your money. I'll sleep in Grand Central Station before I ever take a dime from you." Brent snatched his jacket off the ground. "No, I did it to teach you a lesson. Plain and simple." He jerked his chin toward the bed. "I had no idea you'd be such an eager student."

"Oh, fuck off, Florence." She yelled as he reached the living room. "Don't let the door hit you on your well-spanked ass on the way out."

"Your concern is touching, sweetheart. Miss you already."

He wrenched open the front door and walked into the night.

•••

Hayden pushed open her window and let the cool air off the Hudson blow across her overheated skin. Pressing her palms to her cheeks, she tried to banish the sting of humiliation, but couldn't seem to manage it. If she made it through a single day for the rest of her life without seeing a replay in her mind of what had just taken place, she'd consider herself lucky. In some kind of weird *Pretty Woman* role reversal, she'd offered a man money, moments after sleeping with him. Brilliant.

For a split second, before he'd transformed back into her adversary, she'd caught a flash of hurt move across his features. God, that bothered her. She couldn't stop thinking about it.

She'd just been at such a loss over how to proceed. Standing at the end of her bed, he'd looked at her as though he wanted something more, but didn't know how to ask for it. Maybe she'd *wanted* that thing to be her, but his flippant, sex-is-no-big-deal attitude told her she was wrong. He'd practically jumped out of bed to get away from her, so why would she assume he wanted to stay? Why had she *wanted* him to stay?

Dammit. Just dammit. She'd made a huge mistake in judgment. Not just by offering him money. *Cringe*. Bringing him here. Thinking they could be mature enough to scratch the itch and move on. That had been her mistake. Now she'd made herself look like the materialistic dingbat he'd assumed her to be. But worse, *so* much worse, the pigheaded jerk had rocketed her into another stratosphere in bed. Going into this ill-advised endeavor, she hadn't known what to expect. Would sex with Brent be awkward since they hated each other? Would he simply lie on top of her and work out his own lust like the men of her experience? None of the above. He'd let *her* take the lead. Mostly. It hadn't been easy for him, letting her set the pace, but he'd known exactly how to encourage, to force a response from her without being patronizing or obvious.

Hayden had discovered something about herself tonight. At first, she thought she'd merely been missing control. And she *certainly* had. Taking the reins had put air in her lungs. Purpose in her belly. However, she'd been just as turned-on when Brent flipped her onto her back and dominated her. She suspected because, in her mind, she knew that with Brent, she always retained some level of control. Top or bottom, he listened to her. Wanted to give her what she needed.

The man she'd always assumed took the title for biggest self-centered asshole in the universe was actually a perceptive, unselfish lover. What a kick in the ass. In the past, she'd been treated to polite, non-sweaty sex. No wonder she'd found it overrated. Not anymore. Now she knew how amazing it could be. Yet the thought of being so uninhibited with anyone besides Brent felt...wrong. He'd made her feel safe and desirable. He'd lost his control, too, in the process. She didn't think it would be very easy to find that with someone else.

Swallowing the lump in her throat, she moved to close the window, then jumped when she heard footsteps in the living room. Her heart leaped before she could stop or analyze her reaction. Had he come back? She went to her bedroom door and pushed it open.

"Mother?" She yanked her robe tighter. "What are you doing here? It's almost midnight."

She set her purse down, cast a look into the bedroom behind Hayden. "I needed to speak with you and it couldn't wait until morning." A sigh whistled past her lips. "Obviously you couldn't *wait* either. I met your date sneaking out like a thief in the night."

Hayden pushed her hair over her shoulder, wincing at the thought of Brent running into her mother. Had they exchanged words? She didn't even want to know. "I'm a big girl, Mother. I don't have to account for my every move to you." She dropped down on the couch. "What did you need to talk to me about?"

Her mother picked a piece of lint off her jacket. "I just thought you should be aware of how your actions tonight might have indirectly sent this family into bankruptcy."

Heart pounding in her ears, Hayden shot to her feet. "Excuse me?"

Mother replaced daughter on the couch. "I certainly

hope he was worth it."

She took a deep breath, attempting to calm her racing pulse. "Please, stop being dramatic for one second and explain what you said. Bankruptcy?"

"Gladly." She gestured for Hayden to take a seat across from her. Feeling numb, Hayden obeyed without protest. "Dear, I haven't been pushing Stuart on you because of his sparkling personality. Believe it or not, there *is* a method to my madness." She sighed heavily. "Your father wouldn't like me telling you this. He thinks he can fix it without anyone's help, but I know better. The company has had three bad quarters in a row. We're losing investors and clients by the day. Barely treading water. We've managed to keep it quiet, but your father can only call in so many favors."

"Oh my God." Hayden's hand flew to her throat. Her first thought was for her poor father, having to shoulder the entire burden on his own, keeping a brave face throughout. "What does Stuart have to do with any of this?"

"Stuart, for all his…quirks, is very successful at what he does. His hedge fund is growing by the day, but not fast enough for his liking. He needs the big-time investors. Connections. And that's where your father comes in." She leaned forward. "Unlike Stuart, we're old money, dear. We can introduce him into an invaluable world. And in exchange, he would pay off the hefty loan your father has coming due. If we default on that loan…" She patted her hair. "Let's just say none of us will be living the lifestyle to which we've become accustomed."

Hayden's brain scrambled to keep up. She didn't like where this revelation was heading. Not at all. So she delayed the inevitable. "That's great news, right? If Stuart is going to pay off the loan, what's the problem?"

Her mother took her hand. "Stuart thought he could use your father's connections for free, dear. And you know your father, he's too kind. He'd help Stuart without a thought for himself. Or us." She sat a little straighter. "I finally managed to convince your father that influence doesn't come without a price. Unfortunately, Stuart is looking for a guarantee on his investment."

Dread curled through her body at the direction this conversation had taken. She'd never thought her father belonged in the cutthroat business world. He'd managed to survive this long running a company he'd inherited, but how much longer could he keep it up? If their family lost everything, he would be crushed. "Mother, please just say it."

She nodded once, going from motherly to businesslike. "Stuart came from nothing. Paltry introductions from your father won't give him instant credibility, but linking himself more firmly to the Winstead name *will*. He has a great fondness for you, Hayden. He's agreed to pay off the loan only if you marry him."

Hayden's stomach bottomed out. Even though she'd seen the bombshell coming, it still hit like a well-placed blow. None of it seemed real. This morning, she'd woken up to her neatly ordered life. Before Brent had swaggered in and blasted holes in her perception of herself, of everything. Now, her freedom was in danger of being snatched away. A marriage of convenience. They still happened frequently in her world, but she'd never expected to be part of one. No, this couldn't be happening.

"This came as a surprise to me, too, you know. I was blindsided when I saw our bank statement and realized how much of our family money he's already sunk into fixing the problem. Millions upon millions. Gone. Of course, he refused to touch any of *your* charity accounts."

Her mother watched her carefully. Hayden knew her horror must be showing on her face, because she finally went in for the kill. She spoke very quietly, but her words stung like little bees all over Hayden's body. "Dear, I'm sure I don't need to remind you what your father did for us all those years ago. Where we would be without him. Frankly, we owe him." She clutched her purse in her lap. "Your father knows nothing of this, mind you, and we need to keep it that way. He'd be devastated if he knew I'd burdened you with this."

Yes, Hayden thought dully, she did owe him. It was the only reason she'd even entertained the idea of marrying Stuart this long. Her father, her *paternal* father, was long dead. Two brothers had inherited millions of dollars and Winstead Investments, but only one had shouldered the responsibility of running it. The other had taken his half of the money and blown it on bad investments, partying, and women. She'd been the product of a one-night stand, back when her mother was a college student. Her father had overdosed before Hayden had been born, and her mother had been left behind with an unwanted pregnancy. She'd come to Hayden's now-father, begging for help. After a paternity test, he'd taken them both in, adopting Hayden in the name of respectability. *Blood is blood*, she imagined he'd said. After all, she'd only been a baby at the time. But she knew this story by heart as her mother brought it up whenever it became necessary to keep her in line.

"Hayden?"

She stared at the floor. "How much time do I have to decide?"

"One week. You have one week."

Chapter Eight

Hayden flopped back onto the cracked leather seat and signaled the bus driver to drive. Quickly. Before one of the three dozen kids behind her on the bus remembered they needed to pee or say another final goodbye to their parents. Deborah, the other volunteer for today's expedition, dropped into the seat across the aisle, looking equally shell-shocked. Hayden had made this trip to a farm upstate as part of her Clean Air charity once a week throughout the entire summer, the goal being to take underprivileged kids out of the polluted city for the day, giving them a chance to experience life outside of Manhattan. Today marked their last trip of the season and she still hadn't discovered a way to load the excited kids onto the bus without it turning into a three-ring circus. *Did that make her the ringleader or a clown?*

Her relieved exhale was lost among the shouting and laughter coming from the back of the bus, but she couldn't deny feeling a sense of accomplishment. She'd watched the children flourish over the summer, working with animals and spending time around nature. While Hayden preferred the city, she'd never once felt trapped by limited financial resources, as if she couldn't leave. Her family's frequent vacations had made sure of that. Yet she was painfully aware that she could have easily been one of these kids if it weren't for her father. As always, the reminder of her father's selflessness caused an invisible weight to press down on her shoulders. Only now it felt twice as heavy.

She'd had a difficult time sleeping last night. After having her mother drop the Stuart bombshell on her, she'd been kept wide-awake by the possibility of an arranged marriage. It certainly didn't help matters that she suddenly wanted a man she despised, or *should* despise, rather. Time had flown while she pondered her fate, tossing and turning in bed, the ticking clock on her decision already speeding by in a blur. Sometime around 3:00 a.m., Hayden thought she had the crisis solved. Her mother mentioned her father's reluctance to use the money set aside in her name. She would just have to convince him otherwise.

Unfortunately, she'd promised her mother not to betray their conversation to her father, putting her back at square one. Marrying Stuart. One week left her little time to attempt much else.

Even with such a heavy choice occupying her mind, the memories of her night with Brent refused to fade. An image of his intense expression as he drove into her swam through her head. *Brent.* Damn. Just thinking his name made her feel hot and anxious. Her body buzzed, begging for more of the stimulation he'd provided. More of what she might very likely never experience again. No, she had to stop thinking in terms of mights and maybes. They weren't traveling down that orgasmic road ever again. Even if she somehow got out of marrying Stuart, she didn't want to engage in a physical relationship with someone who couldn't see past her lifestyle to the person underneath. Having sex with someone who disliked her and everything she represented made her feel used. Hurt. Something she wasn't expecting.

Regardless of her damaged feelings, she'd been unable to go five minutes without thinking about him. Then almost immediately, thoughts of the conversation with her mother would intrude and thinking of Brent would start to hurt for an entirely different reason. A cycle she could really do without.

The bus jerked and sputtered, shooting Hayden forward in her seat. *What the hell?* Their driver met her eyes in the rearview mirror and shrugged. Always a comforting sign. Even less comforting? When the bus made an eerily human-like groan and coasted to a stop on the side of the West Side Highway. Hayden sat glued to her seat for a moment, waiting for some divine intervention to save them. After casting a panicked glance at Deborah, she twisted around in her seat. Traffic on the highway was already backing up. Horns honked. Drivers snaked past shaking their heads. For once all the kids were completely silent, all wearing disappointed expressions, no doubt thinking this unforeseen disaster meant they would miss their last week escaping the city.

Then all at once, those sad expressions focused on her. Oh God, they were all counting on her and she'd maxed out her skill set organizing the outing and loading them onto the bus. Judging from their faces, it was painfully obvious, even to the group of fourth graders, that their leader was sorely lacking.

"Shoot," Hayden muttered under her breath. She rose and went to the driver. "Do you know how to fix this thing?" He didn't even have the grace to answer. Simply shook his head and climbed off the bus to light a cigarette. She took a deep breath and dug her cell phone out of her pocket. Ten minutes later, she got through to someone at roadside assistance. "An hour?" She practically shouted into the receiver. "I'm in a bus with thirty-six kids blocking a lane on the West

Side Highway. Does impending mutiny really not count as an emergency?" The unhelpful voice on the other end went silent, obviously not finding amusement in her harried joke. She heaved a breath. "Okay…look, just forget it. I'll figure something else out."

"They say an hour," Deborah chimed in when Hayden hung up, "but look at the traffic behind us. It'll take a tow truck two hours just to get through to us."

Super helpful, Deborah! A Nerf football flew past her and got lodged on the dashboard. Restless energy became a tangible thing on the bus. Hayden knew she needed to figure out something quick. It appeared she was on her own in resolving this problem. She knew what she needed to do, but her reluctance to call Brent and give him the satisfaction made her dial his number extra slowly. Before he even answered, she was already irritated with him.

Brent answered sounding amused. "We're going to need a bigger boat."

Even in her annoyed state, she couldn't help but feel a hint of relief that he hadn't ignored her call after their argument the night before. "What are you talking about?"

"Your personal ringtone is the *Jaws* theme song."

Hayden smirked as if he could see her. "Can't see how that makes any sense. *Jaws* had a sequel. We won't."

"Oh, yeah? Then why are you calling?"

Shit. Just say it. "Try to keep the gloating to a minimum, but I need your…help."

"What's wrong?"

She was momentarily thrown off by how instantly and genuinely concerned he sounded. Why couldn't he just gloat and make this easier for her? "Oh, not much. I'm broken down in a bus on the West Side Highway. With a bunch of kids who are about to go *Lord of the Flies* on my ass."

"That's *you*?" He cursed under his breath and she could

hear the sound of tires squealing in the background. "They already sent over a car. They're having to reroute traffic. You're causing major delays, duchess."

"Not helping."

"I'm on my way," he assured her, adding, "Don't go anywhere."

"Couldn't resist, could you?"

• • •

Lights flashing on the top of his Emergency Service truck, Brent pulled to a stop in front of the stationary yellow school bus, wondering not for the first time what the hell Hayden was doing on a bus with schoolkids. He radioed dispatch to alert them that he'd arrived on the scene, then climbed out of the vehicle, immediately searching through the windshield for Hayden. He'd been hungry for a glimpse of her since last night, but he'd never imagined it would be under such odd circumstances. A motorist passed the bus, blaring his horn, and Brent sent him a dark look.

That pretty much summed up his mood since leaving her bed the previous night.

She'd thrown him for a goddamn loop, after which he'd been treated to a nice little put-down by her mother on the way out. For a brief second, he'd actually felt sorry for Hayden. Mommy Dearest appeared to be about as maternal as a cobra. Not that he expected Mom to embrace him and invite him to her next women's luncheon. After all, he'd just walked out of Hayden's town house, hair all fucked-up, shirt untucked, with a look on his face that clearly said, *Pardon my appearance, I just plowed your daughter.* She'd looked him over and sniffed her judgment. *Well, I guess we're all entitled to a few mistakes now and again,* she'd said, clearly pegging him as said mistake.

After that little heartwarming confrontation, one thing had been abundantly clear. He'd made the right decision in leaving. Prior to that, he'd felt slightly conflicted about walking out, thinking maybe he'd overreacted. Her actions hadn't seemed malicious or intentionally baiting. Then he'd been reminded by her mother why they'd wisely agreed to limit their physical relationship to one night. He didn't need these people making him feel like gum on the bottom of their polished shoes. And she clearly wanted nothing more to do with him now that she'd gotten her fill.

None of his rationalizations, however, did a thing to calm his constant, consuming craving for her. Her total abandonment, her screams of pleasure, drowned every other intelligent thought out until he only had the ability to think of next time. What he'd do to her, say to her, to get her wet. How many times he could make her come before finding his own release. Pointless thoughts, since she'd made it clear it was a one-time thing. Thoughts that wouldn't give him a moment's peace, all the same.

The bus door opened and Hayden climbed out. Brent's eyebrows shot up. He'd never seen Hayden in shorts and sneakers. Ever. With her hair pulled back in a ponytail, she looked so damn sweet and innocent, it brought him up short. Her white T-shirt read Clean Air Initiative 2013, her father's company logo beneath. In an attempt to hide his reaction, he strode back to his ESU truck and pulled his emergency mechanic's tools out from under the passenger-side seat. "You're lucky I have these with me," he called over the honking traffic. "I lent them to a buddy last week and he returned them this morning. They'd normally be at home."

"Yes," she replied, exasperation in her voice. "You have my undying gratitude, officer."

Brent turned with a sarcastic rejoinder on his lips,

but when he saw her up close the words died in his throat. She looked...exhausted, eyes puffy with dark smudges underneath. Her usual radiance dulled by pale skin and a tired expression. As if she'd been crying. Why had she been crying? Please God, not because of him or what they'd done. Or how he abandoned her when she'd possibly wanted him again. He wanted to question her. Demand answers. But like an idiot, he'd agreed not to discuss their night together ever again. Where the hell did that leave him?

When she cleared her throat uncomfortably, Brent realized he'd been staring at her without speaking. Her expression was decidedly closed off, telling him that he wouldn't be appeasing his curiosity any time soon. With a case of reluctance, he skirted past her toward the bus. "All right, let's see what's—" Brent lifted the hood and steam poured out. "Well, that's promising."

Hayden buried her face in her hands with a groan. "Take me to the closest bar?"

"Don't start lining up imaginary shots just yet." He set his steel toolbox down on the concrete. After waving away most of the steam, he propped the hood open and peered inside. Checking various sections of the engine for the part requiring repair, he strove to keep his voice casual. Even though, with her standing so close, he felt anything but. "So what are you doing on a bus? Not exactly your typical mode of transportation."

"Yeah, well, my stretch Hummer is in the shop."

Brent glanced over, caught off guard by Hayden's uncharacteristically self-deprecating tone. Her worried gaze was fixed on something in the bus windshield. He followed her line of sight and saw at least twenty preteens, faces pressed against the glass, watching them intently. One of the girls waved at her and she returned the gesture with a shaky smile.

"Are you gonna fix it, Miss Hayden?"

Her throat worked as she looked toward Brent for an answer. That look impacted him like a blow to the chin. She needed him. It was right there in her expression. *Fix it, Brent.* That look called to the provider inside him, twice as amplified around Hayden. He needed a moment to rein it back in. Before she glimpsed the vulnerability and ripped him to shreds over it. He was saved by the kids yelling once more through the glass.

"We're going to be too late to milk the cows!"

"Tell that cop to show us his gun!"

Apparently the surprises weren't over. "Did he just say 'milk the cows'?"

She nodded without meeting his eyes. "We're taking them up to Meadowstar Farm for the day. They have cows there. Moving on."

Everything clicked into place then. Clear Air Initiative. Even Brent had heard about the popular charity on the local news. He'd had no idea Hayden was involved in any way, but based on the company logo on her shirt and the kids' obvious comfort with her, she'd committed herself to the cause. How long had she been shuttling these kids upstate without him having a single clue? Brent had too many questions, so he started with the most pressing. "Do *you* milk the cows?"

"Yes." Her face softened slightly. "Once. My hands were too cold. Bessie was *udderly* pissed."

Hiding his smile, Brent crouched down to remove tools and a spare quart of antifreeze from his box. Dammit, the need to kiss her wouldn't go away. It was difficult to ignore when they were taking shots at each other. Now? When she stood there in her pristine white Converse, hitting him with more goofy wordplay? It was damn near impossible. And it reminded him of his all-too-brief time in her bed. *Focus.* "All right, *Miss* Hayden. It looks like you've got an antifreeze leak coming from one of your hose clamps."

"Solid."

She cast another concerned look at the hovering students, several of them giving her a thumbs-up in encouragement. They looked at her as if she were invincible, Brent thought, but she clearly didn't see it. At the moment, she appeared too focused on this failure, which was totally out of her control. Suddenly, it became imperative to him that she see what those kids saw.

Brent jerked his chin at her. "All right, woman. Get over here."

"What?"

"Get under the hood. You're going to make this repair so you can go milk Bessie on time."

"Me? Are you crazy?" Brent gave her a level look and she held up a hand. "Forget I asked."

He took Hayden's arm and pulled her in front of him. The words stuck in his throat for a moment, she felt so perfect backed against his chest, her scent teasing his senses. "Stand on the front bumper," he instructed gruffly. "I'll talk you through it."

With a deep breath, she took the wrench, white rag, and utility knife he offered, then boosted herself up onto the bumper. Unable to resist the opportunity to touch her, he braced her legs with his body to keep her steady. "If this is a ploy to ogle my butt, learn to pick your moments."

"Not to worry. I'm too focused on your legs."

She sighed heavily. "Okay, Flo, what am I looking for?"

Knowing she couldn't see him, Brent grinned at the nickname. "See that clamp with steam coming out around it? Use the wrench to loosen it. Then pull out the leaky hose using the rag. Don't touch it directly or you'll burn your fingers." While she worked, Brent pointed toward Hayden and gave the kids a thumbs-up, shaking his head in disbelief as though he couldn't believe what a great job she was doing. They high-fived in response.

"Done. I can see the leak."

"Good. Now…this is really important. Grip the hose tight. And *stroke* it."

"You realize I'm holding a heavy metal object, right?"

He swallowed his laugh. "Use the knife to cut off the damaged part of the hose. Once you've done that, reattach the newly cut end. Make sure the clamp is tight."

She had to bend at an angle to get close enough to cut the hose. Brent bit back a groan when her pert ass went up in the air, inches from his face. Her black shorts rode high enough that he could see that ripe area of skin just beneath her tush. If they weren't in plain view of the highway and thirty-odd children, he would have raked his teeth over that smooth flesh, then ripped the damn shorts off to get a better look. "Duchess, I feel it's only fair to inform you, I'm now looking at your butt."

"Enjoy it while it lasts."

"Planning on it."

"You know what I meant," she snapped. "Enjoy looking now because you won't be seeing it again in the near future."

"I heard you. I choose to interpret it differently."

"I'm finished."

"Already? I've barely even touched you yet."

Her body straightened on a disgusted groan. Brent, for what seemed like the hundredth time this week, whispered a heartfelt good-bye to Hayden's ass. "Think you can you manage to help me down without groping me?"

"Can I or will I?"

"*Brent.*"

"Fine. Down you go." He pulled her off the bumper, but couldn't resist hooking an arm beneath her knees and cradling her against his chest for a moment. She started to protest but the loud cheering from the bus cut her off. He didn't take his eyes off her as her expression slowly transitioned from annoyance to astonishment. "Miss Hayden saves the day," Brent observed casually, setting her on her feet. He could feel her watching him as he quickly poured in the quart of antifreeze to replace what had leaked out, then closed the hood and signaled the driver to start the engine. When it roared to life, the excited cheers only increased.

On the way back to his ESU truck, Hayden stopped him with a hand on his arm. His skin burned beneath her touch. Damn, why did she have to look so pretty? "Hey. Thank you. For whatever that was."

"That was all you, duchess." His damn radio crackled on his shoulder. He wanted to throw it into the Hudson just so he could stand there with her a minute longer. It figured that he'd gone the entire morning without one incident on his patrol shift, only to be called away now. "I've got to go," he said reluctantly.

She nodded and stepped back. As he pulled into traffic, heading toward an incident involving a boat collision that might require underwater search and rescue, he watched in the rearview mirror as the kids on the bus greeted her with a group hug. Just how many layers were there to Hayden Winstead? God, he hoped he hadn't lost his chance to find out.

Chapter Nine

Hayden squinted to make out the colorful dartboard, biting her lip in the hopes it would make the thing clearer. When the single board suddenly had a twin, she made a sound of frustration, waving the dart in her friend Ruby's general direction.

"What trickery is this? Are you a dart hustler, too?"

"No," Ruby said, then threw back a shot of tequila. "You're terrible all on your own."

"I make up for it in spirit."

"Your spirit is causing property damage." Ruby gestured to the scatter of darts lodged in the wall around the board.

Hayden fell into her chair with a snort, knocking over an empty glass in the process. Troy, Ruby's boyfriend, worked with Daniel and Brent on the force, which allowed the girls to meet Ruby over beers one night in Quincy's. They'd absorbed the reformed pool hustler into their twosome without missing a beat. Since Daniel and Troy were occupied for the night watching the Mets game with Brent, she'd kidnapped Story to meet up with Ruby at one of her old pool haunts, a gigantic warehouse-style bar complete with a handful of pool tables and a dance floor. Die-hard regulars and college students mixed together to create an eclectic atmosphere. Pool balls cracked, glasses clinked, and laughter punctuated the air. When they'd arrived, classic rock was blaring from the speakers, but had since been replaced by nineties pop anthems, played for the sake of irony.

She'd needed this. Needed not to think. A night to let everything with Brent, with her family, with Stuart, float away in a bathtub of tequila.

Thankfully, she had friends who didn't pester her with questions about her odd behavior or uncharacteristic decision to party like a rock star on a Thursday night. Good thing, since she didn't feel quite ready to share the Stuart Conundrum, as she'd been referring to it in her head. Her friends would yell, scream, and curse like sailors on her behalf, outraged over the idea of Hayden's being forced to get married against her will. While some support might make her feel better in the moment, it wouldn't solve the problem. Nothing would.

"Where is Story?"

Ruby pointed beyond Hayden's shoulder. She turned and saw her best friend soft-shoeing with an older gentleman, laughing like a lunatic. Hayden turned back to Ruby with a questioning look. Ruby shrugged. "He's teaching her how to tap dance."

"Oh." She drained another shot. "Fair enough."

Ruby pulled her phone out of her pocket and checked the screen. "Uh-oh. I'm getting the Troy Bennett Booty Call."

Story fell into a chair next to Hayden. "Daniel just texted me to come over. Are we wrapping up this little shindig any time soon?"

Hayden did a double take. "Did you two just get simultaneous booty calls?"

"The Mets must have won tonight."

"Mmm-hmm," Story agreed into her drink. "You want to share a cab?"

"Whoa, whoa, whoa." Hayden tilted on her chair. "That's it? Girl's night out is finished just cause some baseball team used a thing...to hit a ball...out of the thing." She shook her head. "You know what I'm trying to say."

"No idea."

"I'm lost."

"Oh, well, let me clear it up for you." She paused for drama. "You guys are dick-whipped."

Story gasped. "Not cool, Hay."

"If anything, that description just made this booty call even more appealing," Ruby said.

"Accusations aside," Story continued as if Ruby hadn't spoken. "I have to teach a class of Manhattan's finest kindergartners tomorrow morning. Nothing gets by these kids. They're just waiting for me to slip up." She reached for Hayden's drink. "They're like miniature therapists, silently taking notes. Diagnosing me behind their juice boxes."

"Call in sick." Hayden took a breath. "You guys, I need this."

Her friends exchanged a curious glance. It would be too easy to spill everything out onto the table when they were too drunk to remember the details tomorrow morning. But it wouldn't make her feel better and it would obligate them to stay out drinking when they'd rather be home with their boyfriends.

"What's going on?" Story turned in her seat. "I *thought* something felt off."

"It's nothing," she hastened to say. "It's just been a crazy week. First, my mother tasked me with organizing another charity ball, then I got a leaky hose on the West Side Highway—"

"Huh?" Both girls asked at the same time. Hayden

quickly gave them a rundown of her West Side nightmare and Brent's subsequent roadside assistance. She left out his innuendo-laced directions and blatant ass-gazing. *And* the fact that she'd spent every moment since imagining a very different outcome. One not involving thirty children. One where he shows up with his toolbox shirtless and well…gives her a tune-up in the back of his ESU truck. The temperature in Hildebrand's suddenly felt sweltering.

There he went again. Popping into her head and kick-starting her libido when he should be the furthest thing from her mind. If she married Stuart, he probably wouldn't take very kindly to her fantasizing about Brent. A man who'd threatened him in his own kitchen.

Marrying Stuart would mean less time with Story and Ruby and the guys. No more Saturday nights bantering over cheap beers for her. Not when she'd be expected to appear on Stuart's arm at every high-society function, introducing him as her successful new husband.

Her heart clenched at the realization.

"Yikes. I hope you're planning on switching bus companies for next summer."

Hayden picked up a discarded lime and plunked it into an empty shot glass. "Actually…no. I'm, uh, going to hire five *more* buses. I want to expand the program." She realized her hands were fidgeting so she folded them in her lap. On the ride from Manhattan to the farm, she'd been struck by inspiration, spending the two-hour ride outlining plans to present to the Clean Air committee. The charity would need an influx of funds, but she'd never felt more confident that she could pull it off. No matter what happened with her father's company, with the charity's popularity and reputation, she could find other donors. When she'd walked onto the bus after repairing the engine, she'd felt amazing. Like she could accomplish anything. Fix an engine. Build an even more successful charity. As much as she didn't want to admit it, Brent had played a role, encouraging her without realizing it.

Story squeezed her hand. "Hayden, that's amazing. Why didn't you say anything?"

She brushed off the question. "It's still in the early planning phase."

"Well, with you in charge, five buses is only a start," Ruby said. "Nice job."

Not knowing how to handle the compliment, Hayden only smiled in response. Lately, she'd started wondering if people saw more in her than she did herself. While she didn't want to let herself hope they were right, the decision to expand the program so close to her heart gave her a sense of purpose. It felt good. Once again, she thought back to helping Brent repair the bus, as if she could pinpoint the exact moment her self-confidence had been given a much-needed boost. Even so, she couldn't help feeling a flash of bitterness over the timing. Just as she was coming into her own, her independence could suffer a major setback if she married Stuart. Not to mention, her rocky relationship with Brent…

Brent again. Why wouldn't he go away?

As if synchronized, both Story and Ruby's phones buzzed on the table. To her friends' credit, neither one of them paid their devices the slightest bit of attention. Hayden took pity on them, however, even as her heart swelled that they would stay out all night if she needed to talk. She hiked her purse over her shoulder and stood.

"Come on, guys. We can't have you late for Troy Bennett and Daniel Chase booty calls. It would be sacrilege."

"Are you sure?" Story gained her feet, wobbling noticeably, telling Hayden she would need to take her friend directly to Daniel's door. Knowing Brent would be there, too, she did her best to temper the warring dread and excitement in her belly.

"Ruby, you prop her up while I call a cab."
"Go teamwork."

...

Brent and Troy stood in the lobby of Daniel's building, still talking about the Mets game that had ended an hour earlier. Daniel had come downstairs under the pretense of seeing them off, though Brent suspected he was just growing anxious for Story to arrive. Troy grew surlier by the second as he waited for a call from Ruby to tell him she'd gotten to his place, just around the corner from Daniel's Upper East Side apartment. As for Brent? He should have headed back to Queens an hour ago, but knowing Hayden made up the trio of girls, he'd begun inventing excuses to stick around.

"Why don't you two Nancys turn your phones off and go to bed? I guarantee they wouldn't keep you waiting so long next time."

Troy snorted. "That method won't work with my girl. She'd have me for breakfast." He paused. "Come to think of it, your plan might not be half-bad."

"Excellent advice, Brent." Daniel shook his head. "This must be why you're beating off the women with a stick."

Brent didn't take the bait, falling silent as he thought of Hayden for the tenth time that hour. If she called him right now and asked him to come over, he'd be knocking on her door before she hung up the phone. He wouldn't have the willpower to resist. Alternating images flashed in his head as though projected on a movie screen. Hayden in her tight skirt and stockings, eyeing him with distaste. Hayden swollen-lipped and rumpled, giggling into her pillow. Hayden awestruck as a busload of students applauded her efforts. Which one would she be tonight if he went to her? He didn't give a damn. He just wanted to see her, but he'd fucked his chances their first night together. Even when he'd helped her repair the bus, she'd made it perfectly clear his hands weren't welcome on her body. But God, the idea of not touching her again made him feel sick and anxious.

Daniel, perceptive as always, jumped all over his failure to issue an idiotic comeback. "Uh-oh. Someone's holding back." His expression turned disbelieving when Brent still didn't respond. "Whoa. Since when do you ever hold back?"

"Since you two started telling your girlfriends every damn thing," Brent said, thinking fast. "I feel like I'm part of the Babysitter's Club. You two are like Stacey and Dawn."

"First of all, you know way too much about the Babysitter's Club," Troy interjected. "Second, I call bullshit."

"Complete and utter."

"That's my cue to take off." He slapped them both on the back. "I hope they show up this century."

No sooner were the words out of Brent's mouth than a cab pulled up along the curb. It was like watching the clown car portion of a circus act. One door flung open and Story stumbled out onto the sidewalk, still singing an a cappella version of *Love Shack*.

Hayden and Ruby tumbled out after her, doubled over with laughter, each latching onto Story's arms. "We're just going to get her upstairs," Ruby called to the cab driver. "We'll be right back."

On either side of him, Daniel and Troy crossed their arms over their chests as all three girls stumbled and swayed their way toward the building, beginning the chorus of *Love Shack* all over again. When they caught sight of the men, they ground to a halt so quickly, it was almost comical.

Story blew a strand of hair out of her face. "Busted."

Daniel stepped forward. "I thought you were grading papers?"

"I was at one point…then we went to Brooklyn."

"Ruby," Troy growled.

She threw up her hands. "I'm completely innocent. They came to me."

"You're in big trouble, hustler."

"The good kind or the bad kind?"

"Both."

While the two couples bickered on the sidewalk, Brent locked gazes with Hayden and felt a sucker punch of heat low in his belly. Flushed with intoxication, she looked almost exactly as she had after climaxing around him that first night. Her guard was down again. Why did that get to him so bad? She felt the same urgent need, too. He could tell by the way her lips parted, sucking in a quick breath at whatever she read on his face. Just as quickly, though, she broke their connection, entering herself in the fray.

"This is all my fault. *Please* don't be upset with them. I dragged them out and made them stay way later than they wanted to. Blame me." She hiccuped. Brent struggled against his smile. "They yammered on about you two peaches the whole time and against all odds, they have answered your booty calls. Now, if you'll excuse me, I'll be heading home."

Brent didn't even have to think about it. "I'm driving you."

"That won't be necessary," she countered.

"You can take the ride or I can follow you. Either way, we're going to talk."

"There is precious little for us to talk about."

He arched a meaningful eyebrow at Hayden, who seemed to realize then that all eyes were on them. She'd been adamant about their friends not finding out about them and he wouldn't break that rule tonight. As strong as the urge was to lay claim to her in front of everyone.

After a moment of contemplation, she stomped down the sidewalk. "Fine. Drive me home, Flo."

"Wrong way."

She spun around and marched in the other direction, blowing kisses to Ruby and Story as she passed. Their boyfriends momentarily placated, they both pretended to catch them in midair. "Good night lovelies, it's been real.

Two minutes later, he'd boosted Hayden into his SUV and was driving cross-town toward the West Side. Facing the window, she refused to speak to him. Every time they reached a red light, he couldn't stop himself from looking over at her, remembering what it had been like to have all that pent-up hostility explode around him. When her head fell back against the seat, exposing her smooth throat, Brent had to look away before his eyes could track down over her breasts. He'd have to touch them then, and he wasn't taking advantage of this situation. He desperately wanted to pull over and drag her into the backseat as it was.

Even at this time of night, traffic hindered their progress, but they made it to her town house in under ten minutes. He rounded the SUV to open her door and she practically spilled out into his waiting arms. With a sigh, he hooked one forearm under her knees and carried her up the stoop leading to her door. He wouldn't lie—something about the task, taking care of her, filled him with male pride. "Keys."

"Hmm. Oh, yeah." Hayden rummaged clumsily through her purse and handed him the set. "I played darts tonight." She yawned. "I played darts in Brooklyn."

Brent blinked down at her. Obviously, in her inebriated state, she'd forgotten to be angry with him. Supporting her against his chest, he unlocked the door and pushed it open. "Yeah? How'd you do?"

"Abysmal." She wrinkled her nose at him. "Maybe I should have pictured your face. I'd have hit a bull's-eye for sure."

"Ha. I thought for a second there you'd forgotten to hate

me."

"Nope. I was just pacing myself."

He snorted. "Too bad you didn't have the same idea with the tequila tonight." Brent carried her to the bedroom and set her down on her feet at the edge of her bed.

"How do you know I drank tequila?"

"There's a lime stuck to your shoe."

"No way." She doubled over at the waist to inspect her high heel and collapsed against him with laughter. He steadied her once more, unable to hide his amusement. Goddamn, she was cute as hell like this. When they went out as a group, she normally relegated herself to a strict four-drink minimum. She looked up at him then, all breathless, eyes dancing with humor, and Brent's fight-or-flight instinct kicked in. Her gaze had landed on his mouth and in her intoxicated state, she hid nothing. She wet her lips, moved closer with the clear intention of kissing him. The tenderness he'd been feeling was fast dissipating, replaced with pulse-pounding need.

No, you came here to talk to her. Brent swallowed hard and stepped back. "Uh-uh. Not tonight. Not when you're like this."

"Like what?" He gave her a look, but it only seemed to make her more determined. "Come on. Isn't this why you brought me home?"

"No." She gripped his shirt and pulled him closer. As she rose up on her toes, the tips of her breasts grazed his chest and he groaned. "I'm not doing this, Hayden." Still, when her lips ghosted over his, then returned to sink into a hot, silky, openmouthed kiss, Brent's resolve slipped. He traced her lips with his tongue, starving for the taste he'd been craving for days. She felt soft and willing in his arms, enticing him beyond belief. He wanted with every fiber of his being to boost her up onto the bed and ride out the urgent need, remind her who would always take her home and why.

He opened his eyes to look at her, hoping a visual reminder of her current state would bring him to his senses, but when he saw how tightly her eyes were squeezed shut as she kissed him, something twisted in his chest. She looked as though she were savoring him in equal measure, sending his determination into a tailspin. It took her fingers working his belt buckle to snap him back to reality. He broke the kiss and gently held her away from him.

At first, she looked confused, then her cheeks flamed red. Her hands fluttered at her waist, as if she didn't know what to do with them. Brent cursed under his breath, knowing at the moment she was only capable of seeing this as rejection, when he was really doing it for her. She stumbled a little and he reached out to catch her, but she shoved his hands away. "Get out."

"Hayden—"

"Just get out."

He stared at her a moment, wanting to say more, but rationalizing that she might not even remember what he had to say. She wouldn't want to hear it, either. Having no choice, he turned and left her there, looking stricken. Each step to his car felt more painful than the last.

Chapter Ten

Hayden woke with a scream on Saturday morning when her mattress dipped and shook. She shot up in bed and searched wildly around the dimly lit room for the intruder. *I ought to at least be given the courtesy of seeing my murderer's face before I leave for the sweet hereafter, right?* When she saw Story at the foot of her bed, she deflated with relief.

She pushed her sleep-mussed hair out of her face. "What is the meaning of this? Ryan Gosling was about to go full frontal in my dream." A total lie, by the way. Someone had been about to go full frontal, but it hadn't been Gosling. Much to her supreme irritation, Brent continued to make appearances in her subconscious no matter how much she tried to banish him from her mind.

"Bah. Dreams never deliver on that kind of thing." Story eased a hip onto the bed. "He would have pulled down his pants and there would have been a cantaloupe in place of his peen."

"Hmmm. Either way, its low-hanging fruit."

"Ooh, funny even before coffee. She's the total package."

"Tell it to Gosling."

"I will." She waggled her eyebrows. "If he happens to be in Atlantic City this weekend. Which is where we're going. As in, *now*! Road trip, motherfu—"

"Get out of my room." Hayden pointed at the door. "I venture into New Jersey for no man. Or woman. Even you, blondie."

"I'm not taking no for an answer." Hayden noticed for the first time that Story was immaculately dressed. Before 9:00 a.m. on a Saturday? Unacceptable. "I miss the ocean. The good weather is going to be gone soon and I'm in the mood for some fun."

"Then go screw your hot boyfriend."

"Presently. Oh, I need to tell you about this new thing he did. I had *my* leg back like this—"

"Oh fine! I'm getting up, you fuck monkey."

"Works every time." Story bounded to her feet and fist-pumped. Hayden couldn't help but smile, excitement starting to wiggle its way through her system. Maybe a weekend out of Manhattan was exactly what she needed to clear her head. She hadn't given her mother her decision about Stuart yet, had been putting it off as long as possible. If she decided to follow her marching orders down the aisle, one last weekend of freedom seemed strongly in order.

"So what's the plan? Are we driving or taking the bus from Port Authority?"

"Daniel is driving. If we pack light, all of us should have no problem fitting."

Hayden froze in the process of putting her hair in a ponytail. "Who is 'all of us'?" She'd obviously been at a disadvantage waking up to the news and agreeing before the sleep cobwebs cleared completely, because if she'd actually thought about it for two seconds, she would have assumed Daniel was coming to Atlantic City. No way would he let

Story out of his sight overnight in a strange place, especially after their little foray into Brooklyn. But his car only held four passengers. Who was occupying that fourth seat? She said a quick prayer it wouldn't be the one person she wanted to avoid.

In an attempt to take her mind off her thwarted attempt to drunkenly seduce Brent, she'd worked herself to the bone all day Friday and into the wee hours of the morning. Pounding the pavement, arranging meetings with potential donors for her youth charities by day, drawing up proposals by night. If her father's company, whose name was all over her nonprofit organizations, did tank, money wouldn't come quite so easily and the kids would ultimately suffer. Hayden wanted the coffers flush to avoid any loss of income or skittish donors at all costs.

Story dragged her from her worry. "It's just Brent coming." She winced at Hayden's expression. "Sorry. Matt's on shift, and I tried to get Ruby and Troy along as buffers, but Troy surprised her with tickets to Chicago last night to meet his parents." They both shared a holy-shit chuckle, knowing Ruby would be in all-out panic mode. Probably why Troy, knowing Ruby well, had waited until the last second. "Anyway, we're going to swing through Queens to pick up Brent on the way."

Hayden processed that. She'd not only be spending the weekend in Brent's un-ignorable presence, she would be seeing where he lived. Then sitting in a backseat with him for hours. She wanted to back out, but she already felt too much guilt over leaving her best friend in the dark about Brent. Plus, who knew when she'd have another chance to hang out with the group? Apart from her antagonistic relationship with Brent, they always had a great time together. If she didn't go, she'd regret it.

"Great. I can be ready in an hour."

"Hey hey, what's this?"

"Hmm?" Hayden turned to find Story peering underneath her bed. When she stood, she held up a gigantic men's dress sock. *Brent's* gigantic dress sock, to be precise, obviously left over from Tuesday night. Licking suddenly dry lips, she shrugged casually. "I don't know. Must have gotten into my laundry by mistake."

Story snorted. "Nice try, dude. You been keeping company of the male persuasion and not dishing the details?" She examined the sock. "I mean, this thing could sail a boat. The owner must be one big dude."

Danger zone! Hayden released a high-pitched laugh and snatched the sock away. "Yeah, must be. I wonder if he got one of my pink Hello Kitty socks in exchange."

Her friend looked at her funny for a second, then shrugged and left the room. "I'm putting on coffee," she called over her shoulder. "Pack your bags. Atlantic City isn't going to know what hit her."

Hayden sank down onto the bed. If she'd been going to tell Story about Brent and Stuart, her perfect opportunity had just passed. Now if she ever found out, Story would be hurt that she hadn't confided in her. She debated about barging into the kitchen and spilling everything, but decided against it. No sense in ruining their spontaneous weekend with her personal drama.

Later that morning as they turned the corner of Brent's block, Hayden shifted nervously in the backseat of Daniel's car, watching suburbia pass by in a blur outside her window. As it turned out, Brent lived in a very nice neighborhood. Mothers pushed babies in strollers, children played baseball in the streets. So far removed from her world of imposing brownstones and roof decks, she liked it nonetheless. Could see Brent walking down the street in this neighborhood with a family of his own one day. Why that thought brought on a wave of melancholy, she refused to examine.

They pulled to a stop in front of a brick colonial house with a porch, manicured lawn spanning the front yard. A woman knelt by some potted plants on the steps, holding a watering can. When she saw Daniel exit the car, the woman waved, a huge smile spreading across her face. She looked Brent's age and clearly she was right at home in his house. Hayden sat very still in the backseat until Story pulled her door open and nudged her with a flip-flopped foot.

"Who is that?" she asked quietly.

Story followed her line of vision. "Hmm? Oh, that's Laurie. Brent's sister-in-law." She frowned when Hayden released a pent-up breath. "His brother is army. While he's overseas, Brent helps Laurie with the kids." As if on cue, two towheaded girls ran screaming out onto the lawn. Brent, wearing worn jeans and a Mets hat, chased after them, roaring like a monster. He grabbed both girls around the waist and spun them in the air while they squealed. One of the girls said something that made Brent throw his head back and laugh out loud. The very picture of domestic bliss spread out before her like a panorama of perfection. One she'd always assumed was a myth. One she'd *definitely* never associated with Brent. When she'd pictured his living situation, she'd imagined him passed out among beer cans with the latest copy of *Maxim* forgotten on his chest.

Each squealing towhead took a turn laying a kiss on Brent's cheeks, looking up at him with unabashed hero worship. Hayden's ovaries stood up and delivered a thundering standing ovation. Whoa. *Whoa.* Where had that come from? A loud buzzer went off in her head. The kind you hear in movies before a submarine launches a missile. *First of all, nice to meet you, ovaries. I've heard so much about you. Second of all, fuck right off. You're not welcome here.*

This momentary bout of wistfulness had to be a by-product of her monumental upcoming decision. She'd come to the realization that if she married Stuart, it wouldn't be the marriage she'd always secretly dreamed of. Coffee and conversation in bed. Holding hands while their child performed in some hokey school play dressed as a carrot. Lazy Sunday morning sex. None of it would be coming true. So now, presented with this Norman Rockwell mind-fuck of a vision, the oversensitive woman inside her, the one stuck at the bottom of the well Hayden had pushed her down, was crying out for help. And she wanted to be rescued by the smiling giant who hadn't bothered shaving this morning. The one who'd just caught sight of her across the lawn, and was looking at her with a decidedly odd expression that she couldn't afford to interpret.

At least her ovaries' intervention had been useful in one manner. She could waste no time putting Brent back where he belonged in her mind. Talk about a timely wake-up call.

"Um, Hayden? Did you get bitten by a zombie last night and forget to tell me?" Story waved a hand in front of her face. "If so, we need to have that awkward conversation where I promise to kill you when the change happens."

"No." She shook her head and stepped out of the car. "No killing necessary. And I need to talk to Daniel about the movies he's letting you watch."

...

Brent watched Hayden wander around his living room, perusing family photos and trading small talk with his sister-in-law, who'd stopped by to pick up his nieces and do a few chores around the house as repayment for his babysitting duty. He would have expected her to look out of place in his kid-friendly living room—with crayons and Barbie clothes strewn about on every available surface, they were a far cry from her chic Manhattan town house—but today she hadn't gone for her usual tight, buttoned-up look. She wore one of those dresses. The ones with no straps that hug a girl's breasts, then flow down her body, teasing you with hints of the curves underneath. Her red toenails peeked out just under the hem every time she took a step. All he could think about was those toes digging into his ass while she tightened up around him. Wishful thinking on his part, since she currently wouldn't even look at him. They'd usually exchanged preliminary insults by now. A sinking feeling in his stomach told him something was up, but he couldn't put a name to it.

Life had been so much easier when he didn't know what Hayden tasted like. How she sounded moaning for him to go harder. The way she softened after sex, all liquid-limbed and sleepy-eyed.

Jesus. This was going to be a long weekend.

Frustration clawed at him. Frustration wrought by one sexy stocking enthusiast who, when last he'd seen her, had been in the process of unbuckling his belt. So ready for what he had to offer, she'd been all but panting. Not an easy thing to recover from when you knew where the encounter *would* have led, having experienced it once before. Rough, no-holds-barred fucking. The angry kind that included biting and clawing. Ripping of clothes. Since walking away from her—for the second damn time—he'd been in a state of constant arousal. Nothing helped. Short of finding another woman to work out his lust with, a thought that for some obnoxious reason made him nauseous, he'd tried everything. Lord, he'd taken so many cold showers, he dreaded what his water bill would look like this month.

He suspected this undiluted need for her specifically sprang from his protective nature. This urge to soothe her, when instead he'd been forced to walk away, still lingered days later. It was one thing to trade barbs, but another completely to leave her looking forlorn and humiliated. Because of him. He didn't like it. The memory sat in his gut like lead. Between the constant fantasizing while only wanting the real thing and the uncomfortable feeling that had taken up residence in his chest, he'd been in a perpetually shit-tastic mood.

He really couldn't afford to take off a weekend at the garage. He needed a weekend in Atlantic City like he needed a new pair of pink roller skates.

Laurie's girls took hold of Story's and Daniel's hands and dragged them to the backyard to show off the new tree house he'd built two weekends ago. Brent watched Hayden tense up as she realized they were alone in the room, but he couldn't summon the ability to put her at ease. He needed a moment to collect his own thoughts. Seeing her in his home, so close to his bedroom, made him feel…impatient. He wanted that dress draping down over his thighs as she rode his lap. More than that, he wanted her in *his bed*. Call him a caveman, but he wanted to make her come among his sheets. He wanted to climb into them the following night, remembering the way he'd satisfied his woman there.

His woman? Jesus. She wasn't even speaking to him. On their best day, they were cordial to each other. If she knew he'd laid claim to her in his mind, she would roundhouse him in the nuts. Yet he definitely had. Which was the only reason he'd agreed to this weekend. The thought of her alone in a notorious party-town made him a little crazy. Daniel and Story would inevitably go off on their own, and he meant to be there to make damn certain she went home with him, or no one at all.

Hayden picked up a picture frame and scrutinized it. "This must be your sister."

Her voice hit him below the belt. "How can you tell?"

She set the picture of Lucy in her high school graduation gown back down. "She looks like she can't wait to make somebody's life hell."

A booming laugh escaped him. "That's pretty accurate. She's coming back to New York this summer she finishes grad-school, so you'll find out for yourself."

"Will I?" Something close to longing crossed Hayden's face and he frowned. Again, the feeling that he'd missed a vital piece of the puzzle assailed him. Of course she would have the chance to meet Lucy. No matter what happened between them, they would always have contact with each other. Right? Their group of friends was close. They clicked. Even the constant bickering between them had fast turned into a comfort. Hell, something he looked forward to.

"Yeah." His voice was firm. "You will."

Mouth tight, Hayden nodded. "Great. I look forward to it."

He felt compelled to cross the living room, stand next to her at his fireplace mantel. A wave of her hair shielded her face, frustrating him. What would it take to get a decent look at her face? "Listen, Hayden. The other night…I'm sorry about how it ended. I don't want you to think—"

"Two apologies in one week." Her gaze strayed to his, then drifted away much too quickly. "Are you going soft on me, Flo?"

Oh, screw it. Why did she have to smell so damn good? He moved in close, let his hand drift over her hip. Squeeze a little harder than he should allow himself. "I'm never soft around you, duchess."

She reacted like she'd been burned, but quickly recovered. "If you're waiting for an apology, keep waiting. That's your department, not mine."

"You'd rather go back to fighting? To the constant insults?"

"*Yes.*" Her eyes squeezed shut. When they reopened, he couldn't find Hayden anywhere in the brown depths.

The absence of her fire, her fight, kicked him square in the stomach. "That's us, Brent. That's what we do."

Brent shook his head emphatically and started to respond when the kids scampered back into the living room. He watched Hayden's surprised reaction when the girls grabbed her hands and dragged her toward the backyard. She looked as though she wanted to inform them they were making a mistake. That perhaps they'd grabbed on to the wrong adult, but ultimately she had no choice but to follow.

"Come on! Story and Daniel are turning into zombies and we have to fight them."

Hayden paused. "Ooh. I didn't exactly wear my zombie fighting shoes today." The girls stared down at her feet in disappointment. "Um. So I guess I'll have to take them off?"

"Yay!"

As she was dragged through the back of his house, he heard her say, "You know, zombies don't even eat children. You're way too bony. Terrible for their fragile digestive tract."

Giggles. "You're funny."

"Oh, yeah? Huh."

Trying and failing to ignore the odd pang in his stomach, Brent followed them. He stopped just inside the screen door to watch Story and Daniel chase the girls around his yard, Hayden warding them off with a broom handle. He couldn't afford to have *this* Hayden thrown into the mix as well. One who humored his nieces. It only served to confuse him more.

Better to keep his mind focused on the thing between them that not even she could deny, because he and Hayden weren't finished. Not by a long shot.

The sooner she realized he wasn't fading silently into the night, the better.

Chapter Eleven

Hayden flung her leather travel case onto the hotel room bed and went to stand in front of the air conditioner. Her skin felt flushed, feverish. The two-hour ride from New York to Atlantic City had been absolute hell. Brent had crowded her in the backseat of Daniel's car with his gigantic body, pressing his arm or thigh against her at every opportunity. She'd made a valiant attempt to ignore his interested perusal by staring out the window. Then the whispering had started. After that, her temperature had steadily risen until she felt like a whistling teakettle.

Sure, it had started innocent enough. For Brent. *You look sexy as hell in that dress. You smell fucking amazing.* But when she'd continued to patently ignore him, the rough whispers near her ear went from PG to NC-17 before she could blink. *Duchess, tug the top of that dress down just a little. Just enough that I can sit here and imagine sucking your nipples.* Then there was the one accompanied by his hand squeezing the front of his jeans. *Sit on my lap, baby. I just need your weight* right *here.* Or the one that had nearly melted her into the seat. *If I slipped my hand under your dress right now, no one would know but us. Think you could stay quiet long enough to come?*

When Daniel finally pulled up outside the Borgata hotel and casino, she'd practically dived from the still-rolling vehicle to escape Brent, ignoring the deep chuckle behind her. Oh, but it hadn't ended there. Fortunately, the check-in line had been short. *Un*fortunately, her room and Brent's room were separated only by an adjoining door. It never occurred to her, in a hotel this size, that such a coincidence was possible, so she'd made it all the way to her room, Brent one step behind her, before realizing it. He'd whistled as he unlocked his door, sending her a sly wink as the door slowly closed.

Her insanely hot response to Brent concerned her. Big-time. This weekend would be twice as difficult as she'd imagined it would. At worst, she'd pictured them fighting. Maybe needling each other a little harder than usual. Brent obviously had other plans. He didn't appear satisfied to part ways after one night. She lifted the hair off her neck and blew out a breath. Apparently her body had sided with Brent. And, damn him, he knew it.

What he didn't know? When this weekend was over, she might very well agree to marry someone else. She needed to put an end to this thing between them. One more slipup and it could easily turn into a habit. Into something that clouded her decision-making process. Her judgment. If she married Stuart, happy or not, she would be 100 percent committed to him. It didn't matter that it was a business arrangement. There wouldn't be anyone else once she agreed to be his wife. If she allowed herself more time with Brent, agreeing to marry someone she felt zero attraction for would be twice as difficult.

Hayden's cell phone buzzed in her purse, interrupting her dark thoughts. Her mother. "Hello."

"Where are you? I'm standing outside your house."

She sat at the edge of the bed and kicked off her sandals. A cold shower was definitely in order. "I'm with Story in Atlantic City."

A long pause. "Is *he* there?"

"Who?" Hayden played dumb. "Daniel? Yes. Where one goes, the other follows."

Her mother made an impatient noise. "You know to whom I'm referring. Based on your evasion, I assume he is there." A pregnant pause. "Honestly, you couldn't pick someone more discreet to have one final fling with?"

Hayden straightened. "I haven't made my decision regarding Stuart yet." She unzipped her bag, drew out her toiletry bag. "And you've only met Brent once. I doubt you can vouch for his ability to be discreet."

A snort. "Oh, please. He's a loud, ill-mannered cop who moonlights as a grease monkey. Frankly, it's embarrassing."

She felt a flash of annoyance, followed quickly by the startling realization that her mother wasn't saying anything she hadn't said herself about Brent in the past. Her shoulders slumped under the weight of that thought. "Actually, he's working two jobs because he helps support his brother's family. Plus, his sister in college. Which is kind of…well, it's pretty damn amazing. And he certainly won your friends over the other night. It's not fair to call him ill-mannered." Unbelievable. She'd just defended Brent.

A long-suffering sigh. "I'm going to let you go now. But Hayden, if and when you decide to make the right decision, do make sure Brent knows where he stands. We wouldn't want any loose ends."

After the line went silent, Hayden stripped her dress over her head. Now she needed a shower not only to cool her heated skin, but also to wash away the conversation she'd just had with her mother. She padded to the bathroom, stopping short when she heard two men's voices coming from Brent's room, one belonging to Daniel. After the briefest hesitation, she opened the door on her side and pressed her ear against the smooth, cool wood.

"Danny, sit down." Brent's baritone voice. "You're making me dizzy."

"You think she'll say yes?"

"I don't know..." Brent answered, and Hayden frowned. Perhaps she'd been too quick to defend him. Whatever Daniel planned on asking Story, she had a pretty strong feeling the answer would be yes. "I figure you've got about a fifty-fifty shot."

"Be serious, dick. I'm about to propose here. *Me*. What would you have said if I'd told you that six months ago?"

Daniel was going to propose? Hayden's hands flew up to cover her thrilled smile.

"Six months ago? I'd have told you to seek medical attention immediately because you've received a concussion."

"Exactly. I haven't had a lot of time to work myself up for this. I never thought..." He trailed off. "I never *let* myself think this could happen for me."

A deep sigh from Brent. "You're really going to make me say this Oprah bullshit out loud, aren't you?" She couldn't make out Daniel's muffled reply. "Listen. Story is going to say yes. Why? Because no one in this world loves her more, or knows her better than you. And she knows it. It's all over her face when she looks at you. She found her soul mate."

At the unexpected sincerity from Brent, Hayden's throat constricted. Her eyes filled with moisture. She could practically see both men shifting uncomfortably in the next room and it only touched her more.

"I hope you're happy. Now I have nothing left for my best man toast at the wedding."

Daniel cleared his throat. "I haven't asked you to be my

best man."

"You will."

"Yeah. I know." She heard some shuffled steps, then Brent's hotel room door opening. "Thanks, man. See you at dinner."

"I'm so going to order the manliest fucking steak on the menu to make up for this."

The door closed on Daniel's laughter. Hayden stayed very still with her ear pressed to the door, absorbing what she'd just heard. It was more than just a profound moment between two friends. She'd already been sliding down her mountain of judgment concerning Brent. First when he'd apologized at the dinner party for not preventing an encounter between her and Stuart. Then again this afternoon, seeing him with his nieces. Learning about his daily sacrifice to support his family. For months, she'd thought of him as nothing more than an irreverent jackass. She'd clearly been wrong. But it was too late to matter.

Before the depressing thought could fully form, the adjoining door opened and she tumbled forward into Brent's room. He caught her just before she could face-plant at his feet.

"Eavesdropping, duchess?" His laughter died in his throat when he saw she wore only a strapless bra and panties. His entire demeanor changed from playful to sexually charged in an instant. Muscles tensed, his cheekbones flared red. Swiftly, her body responded to his, sensing the one who could satisfy it. How could she resist this when her brain had so little control?

She must. Her feelings toward Brent were rapidly transforming into something she hadn't anticipated. Being intimate with him would only muddle her brain further. She wouldn't be able to sleep with this fiercely passionate man and then marry someone who paled in comparison. It would make performing her duty to her family unbearable. It would wreck her.

Grasping her tenuous resolve like a lifeline, she tried to skirt past him toward her room. She'd made it to the door when one large hand appeared above her and pushed it closed with a *click*. Tension-filled seconds ticked by. Hayden stood frozen, except for the increasingly fast rise and fall of her chest. When she felt Brent move closer, his muscular chest brushing her back, she bit her lip to hold in a whimper. More than anything, she wanted to press back into him, move her naked skin against his clothes. Entice him with a twist of her hips on his lap. Instead, she squeezed her eyes closed and remained still. Even knowing Brent would let her, she couldn't make herself open the door and return to her room. She simply didn't have that kind of willpower.

"Did I get you all revved up on the ride here?"

Her breath escaped in a rush when Brent's hand skimmed over her hip and came to a rest on her belly, brushing the skin with work-roughened fingertips. Every inch of her body had become so painfully aware of him that she couldn't draw air into her lungs.

"Are you here to make me pay for the bad words I said to you?"

A sound fled her lips, arousal and surprise mixed together. She hated that he knew exactly what to say. Exactly how to make himself irresistible to her. She also craved it. No one had ever understood so thoroughly what she needed. All without an ounce of judgment.

Suddenly, as if something snapped inside him, he lifted her high against the door, levering her there with his hips pressed snugly into her bottom. He worked his bulging erection between her thighs and pushed up hard. Hayden's tiptoes barely skimmed the ground. She had no choice but to brace her palms against the door and relish the unleashed power behind her. All the while knowing he'd hand over control if she simply asked for it. "I have a few more bad words for you. Would you like to hear them?"

"Yes." The whispered word broke free before she could suppress it. Brent rewarded her by slowly grinding his hips into her, growling against her neck as she panted.

He brushed her hair aside with one hand and scraped his teeth down the side of her neck. "You made this fucking sound, Hayden. The first time you spread your legs to take my cock. I hear it everywhere I go. This goddamn…moan? Sob? I don't know. All I know is if I don't fuck that sound out of you again soon, I'm going to completely lose my mind."

Every muscle in her body weakened, went languid. She pressed her forehead against the door in an attempt to anchor herself. Her body screamed at her to take this man inside her. Her reasons for staying away were fast beginning to dissipate from her mind.

She opened her mouth to tell him to let her go. "Is there more?" came out instead.

Brent's pained laugh rumbled in his chest, sending goose bumps down along her arms. "Woman, I could go all day."

He worked himself against her, his jeans creating such incredible friction as they slid along her silk panties that Hayden couldn't control the spreading dampness, the insistent pulsing that grew more demanding by the minute.

"You loved it, didn't you? Cuffing me? Riding me?" He waited for her shaky nod. "Good. You can tie me up and fuck me within an inch of my life, and I'll just beg for more. But so help me God"—he thrust against her so hard her feet inched off the floor—"I'm going to have you just like this someday. I'll surrender to you, over and over, but you'll goddamn surrender to me when I ask. I want to be clear about that."

Her stomach muscles tightened, her chest shuddered as she sucked in a breath. "I guess we'll see about that," Hayden said, fully aware she was playing a dangerous game, but too drugged with arousal to care. She tossed her head back onto his shoulder. As if anticipating her move, his mouth met hers in an all-out battle of lips and tongue. He groaned into her mouth as they fought for control. She circled her bottom on his erection, his hands gripping and guiding her. Setting the pace.

One big hand traveled over her hip to slip down the front of her panties. Adept fingers found her clitoris and massaged, drawing on her dampness to make her slippery.

"Let's end this game now." He shoved two big fingers inside her, crooked and rotated them until she cried out. "You need my cock here. Twice a day." He kissed her hard, thrusting his tongue deep. "I'm a big man, Hayden, and I fuck twice as long, and twice as hard. You'll get used to it. And then you won't be able to stand in the same room as me without wanting a ride."

His thumb found her clitoris once more and applied a perfect amount of pressure. A whimper of pleasure stuck in Hayden's throat. She struggled with the desire to let him release the tension he'd built inside her, give him relief in exchange. With her thighs shaking, her sex clenching, walking away now seemed impossible. Surely she wouldn't survive it. But his words rang in her head, warning her that staying would be a mistake. *Twice a day. You'll get used to it.* Brent was speaking in the long-term. This attraction between them was quickly graduating to something more serious and she couldn't allow it. Once a man like Brent decided something or someone belonged to him, she pitied anyone who stood in his way. With her responsibilities weighing down on her shoulders, Hayden had to stop this or she would never be able to.

"No, Brent. Stop." When the words left her mouth she nearly broke down and cried. As she'd known he would,

Brent ceased all movement as soon as her plea got through. He removed his hand slowly, reluctantly. It made her want to cry all the more. He let her slip down to the floor, but stayed flush against her back. She could feel every inch of him pressed against her and knew he had to be close to his breaking point. In that moment, she hated herself. Hated the obligations preventing her from exploring her intense physical yearning for this man.

"Why, dammit?" He spoke hoarsely at her neck. "We want each other. Tell me why."

When Hayden answered, her throat felt so incredibly tight, it hurt to speak. "It's complicated."

"Try again."

What could she say? *I might marry someone else, someone for whom I feel nothing, in order to retain the wealth you so greatly resent?* He would never understand. Furthermore, he wouldn't hesitate to tell Story and Daniel, who would never let her go through with it. And to top it off, the news would ruin what should be a happy weekend for her friends.

She reached for the doorknob. "I don't want this. Stop trying to force something that isn't there."

When he flinched at her use of the word "force," she felt a painful surge of guilt. Thankfully, she was able to keep it hidden as she yanked open the door and entered her own room. She remained there with her back pressed up against the locked door for long moments, hearing no movement on the other side. Just as she pushed off, heading toward the bathroom, she heard something heavy crash and break in Brent's room.

Chapter Twelve

As all four friends sat down at the round, candlelit table for dinner, an irritable Brent watched Hayden choose the seat farthest from him. He didn't want to look at her, didn't want to care about what "complication" she'd been referring to earlier. In fact, the afternoon spent away from her had given him time to think.

After he'd hurled the Yellow Pages at the wall, accidentally knocking the hotel phone across the room. Along with a coffeemaker.

The girls had gone swimming at the hotel pool and he'd convinced Daniel to join him at the poker tables. Turns out, poker required you to sit quietly for hours on end, something that would normally make him break out in a cold sweat, but he had embraced it wholeheartedly after the scene with Hayden. While he'd waited for strangers to play their hands, he'd resolved to stay away from her. She'd fucked with him for the last time. If she ever decided to stop pretending they didn't set each other on fire, she'd seriously have to woo his ass. And no, he didn't care if that made him sound like a chick.

Now, however, his raging thoughts simmered down from a mighty roar to a pitter-patter of little elves' feet when he saw her in the flesh. All soft and glowing, dressed in her Vacation Hayden getup, he could think of nothing but how she'd looked that afternoon in her bra and panties, skin flushed from the way he'd dirty-talked her in the backseat. She'd fallen through his door looking like sex on a platter and he'd thought, *Christmas came early. Guess I've been a good boy.* They'd been seconds from soul-screaming, mind-blowing, hair-pulling sex. *She'd* kissed *him*. She'd worked her barely covered ass all over him, showing him what he was about to get. Then something he'd said caused her to put the brakes on.

Something about her words, her actions afterward, continued to eat at him all afternoon. He hadn't needed to see her face to see the conflict taking place in her. Her shoulders had been bunched, breathing erratic. Even her verbal parting shot didn't strike him as convincing. So what the hell was the problem? *It's complicated.* If he could go back in time, he'd ask her what the hell in this life *isn't* complicated. Sure, they'd spent the first few months of their acquaintance as enemies. Could that be the extent of it?

No, something else was in play. But as bad as he wanted to put a name to it, his pride wouldn't allow it. He refused to interrogate her. She would have to come to him. He didn't take her accusation of "forcing" himself on her lightly. He suspected she knew that, too.

Determinedly, he tore his gaze from soft, glowing, light-blue-vacation-dress-wearing Hayden and gave his drink order to the hovering waitress.

Across the table, Daniel stared into the candle's flame in front of him, looking as though he might puke.

Enough was enough. Since Story and Hayden were

distracted pointing out menu choices to each other, Brent snapped his fingers in front of Daniel's face.

"Hey, shithead. Look alive," Brent whispered harshly, giving him a disgusted look. "Honestly, I don't even know you anymore. Since when do you worry about getting the girl? Grow a pair, man. You're Daniel fucking Chase. *He who gets the girl*, remember?"

Daniel gaped at him for a moment before rapping his fist on the table. "You know what? You're right."

"You'll have to be more specific," Brent returned. "I'm right so frequently."

"About me. I get the girl." He looked at Story, whose gaze connected with his at the same time, her mouth parting slightly at whatever she read there. "I'll get my girl."

"Great, now that your pussy-whipped-ness is settled, let's eat."

Brent spent the next half hour, as they drank wine and ate appetizers, doing his best not to stare at Hayden. She made it incredibly difficult when every once in a while, just when he thought she'd dismissed him completely from her mind, her increasingly heavy-lidded brown eyes would find him across the table, causing everything below his belt buckle to tighten. He thought of how her mouth would taste after drinking red wine. The red wine she continued to sip in such ladylike fashion. He knew better. If he took her mouth right now, she'd fight him for control. Dig her fingernails into him and rob him of sanity. He wasn't the only one who felt this way. No, the more she relaxed and drank her wine, the more he saw. Not just desire. Vulnerability. The combination pummeled him.

A thought occurred to him. Perhaps his pride wouldn't let him pursue Hayden after this afternoon's latest blue-ball extravaganza, but he could provoke her into coming to *him*. Their first night together had been triggered by a challenge. Whether or not she could teach him a lesson. Whether or not she could handle him. Maybe he'd made it too easy for her today. That ended now. No more Mr. Nice Brent.

Just as he had the idea, Hayden glanced up at him and frowned a little, cluing him in to the fact that he needed to hide his thoughts a little better.

"Hayden!" Story giggled into her wine as Daniel reached across the table to hold her hand. "Tell everyone about the time in college we drove to Mexico. When you rode the donkey."

Brent had to drink deeply when Hayden's face broke into a beautiful smile. It turned her into the girl he'd seen snuggle a pillow, making puns in the dark. Pillow-puns Hayden. Brent expected her to decline to tell the story, make a sarcastic remark, and pass the buck back to Story. But tonight she seemed different. Pensive one minute, sentimental the next. It worried him.

Hayden took one final sip of her wine and set it down with a flourish. "Well. We were bored on a Saturday and Story got a craving for tamales. Since I'd never eaten one, she insisted we road-trip to Mexico on a quest for my perfect first tamale. A little crazy, but since midterms had just ended, we needed to blow off some steam." She nodded at Story. "Of course, this one got us lost and we ended up in some town with no name, a map we couldn't read, and not a tamale in sight."

As if on cue, both men at the table folded their arms and sighed, outwardly irritated by the idea of two college coeds lost in a foreign country. It only made Story and Hayden laugh harder. Even Brent couldn't keep the smile completely off his face, seeing the two girls look so happy.

"We were starving, so we stopped at a fruit stand on the side of a dirt road. Two donkeys were tied up in back. The owner, knowing two suckers when he saw them, told us we could ride them for five American dollars. Before he'd even finished making his offer, Story had climbed onto one of the beasts and named it Maxwell. As you do."

Story took over the telling. "We were only riding for a few minutes when Hayden's donkey started making this horrible braying noise. Like, *the* worst sound you've ever heard. So Hayden got off his back and the poor thing just kind of… pooped out in the middle of the street."

"Then it went into labor."

Story could barely speak through her laughter. "Hayden ran back and got the fruit stand owner, who promptly passed out at seeing a live birth. While I tried to shake him awake, Hayden delivered a donkey baby in the middle of the street. All while sporting an Hermès scarf, by the way."

Brent gaped at Hayden, but she was too busy enjoying herself to notice. Her entire face had lit up, animated in a way he'd never seen her. Or maybe he'd just been blind to anything apart from how she portrayed herself on the surface. Cool and disinterested. But underneath…Jesus, she was so much more. Energy and light just waiting to shine through.

Where the hell had that thought come from? Relationship Daniel had obviously rubbed off on him. But as he'd already realized, subtle coaxing wouldn't work with Hayden. He was going to have to step up his game if he wanted a shot with her.

Resolved to stick with the plan, he tuned back in to the story. "Marco finally woke up after Hayden dumped a gallon of water on his head. He was so thankful that he named the donkey after her."

Hayden raised her glass, smiling at everyone's laughter. "It's true. Somewhere in Mexico, I have a namesake with fur." She sighed. "We never got our tamales."

When everyone's laughter died down, Brent bit the bullet. "So what did they name the donkey? Pampered Princess?"

Her wineglass froze halfway to her mouth. The table went silent. He could feel Daniel's death stare but ignored it. He needed to shake her up, and it couldn't wait another second. True to form, Hayden didn't disappoint. She set her glass down and smiled sweetly. His gut clenched when her eyes lit up, challenging, excited. "Aw, what's wrong, Brent? Jealous? After all, if ever there was someone who deserved to have a jackass named after him, it's you."

He leaned forward on his elbows. "Yeah? And what would they name it? How about…Spanky?"

Hayden's composure slipped a little, but he only noticed because of how closely he watched her. "How about Oversized Dickhead?"

He shrugged. "Didn't hear you complaining about my oversized—"

She shot to her feet, jostling the table. "Can I speak with you in private?"

"You need it right now?" He feigned exasperation. "We're in the middle of dinner, woman. You're insatiable."

Story suddenly ducked down and peeked under the tablecloth, gasping and drawing everyone's attention. "Brent, what size are your feet?"

His brows drew together. "Fifteen. Why?"

"Ahhh!" She pointed an accusatory finger at Hayden, shoving Daniel's shoulder with her other hand. "Sock guy. He's sock guy!"

"Oh yeah, he's going to get socked, all right."

"Brent is sock guy?" The couple exchanged a look. "But wait, you guys hate each other," Daniel protested.

Hayden narrowed her eyes. "Jesus, you really do tell each other everything."

"You owe me," Story continued indignantly. "I've been keeping up my end of the sex talk and I get nothing in return. Nothing! You owe me some details."

Daniel held up single finger. "Wait a minute. You talk to Hayden about what we do in bed?"

Her best friend sank down into her seat and Hayden

sighed. "Oh, relax, Danny. She walks around our apartment humming like a freaking Disney princess. Birds literally perch on her shoulder when we go outside. You should be proud."

Daniel smirked at Story. "Did you tell her about the new leg thing?"

"Oh, for Christ's sake," Brent griped.

Before an awkward silence could settle over the table, Story pushed back her chair and stood. "Why don't we all just get some air?"

...

Brent and Hayden walked in tense silence, trailing Story and Daniel on the boardwalk. The sun had just begun to set, soft music drifted from portable radios on the beach, a soft breeze rolled off the ocean to cool Hayden's skin. It was a beautiful night. Perfect for Daniel's imminent marriage proposal to her best friend.

Hayden wanted to scream.

The man walking so casually next to her actually had the nerve to whistle. *Whistle.* Her willpower had never faced such a powerful test. Without it, she would have already tackled him into the sand, pinned his arms over his head... and kissed the shit out of him. That, *that*, is what had her so angry. She didn't understand her reaction any more than she understood his sudden revelation at dinner regarding their physical relationship. What was his game? Getting back at her for turning him down? Or perhaps Brent thought if he bit the bullet and blurted the news to their friends, she'd have no excuses not to jump into bed with him.

Whatever his reasons, she found her resolve weakening at an alarming rate. He looked edible in his dinner clothes, all raw maleness wrapped up in gray trousers and a loose black dress shirt, barely containing the solid muscle beneath.

His swagger held an extra hint of arrogance tonight, doing precious little to dim his appeal. Her hormones were still performing a sultry tango in her stomach, left over from the drive and the almost-sex in Brent's room. Combined with her frayed nerves, courtesy of her upcoming decision, Hayden felt ready to snap. She felt out of control. She needed *something*. Unfortunately, she had a feeling that *something* was the six-foot-five hormone-whisperer walking beside her, whistling the *Happy Days* theme song.

She couldn't hold on to her irritation anymore. "Stop whistling, Flo. You're scaring people. When a man your size whistles, he's just chopped up half the cast of a horror film."

Without missing a beat, he started whistling the theme song to *Halloween*.

"Oh, real cute." She whipped off her sandals so she could walk barefoot and felt a surge of satisfaction when his whistling stuttered. Huh. Brent was a foot man. Go figure. "I don't know what you were hoping to accomplish back there, but it didn't work."

"Did it piss you off?"

"Oh, yes."

"Well, then. Mission accomplished." He shrugged. "After all, that's what enemies do, right? Piss each other off? And I'd say dinner just won me the gold medal at the piss-your-enemy-off-Olympics."

Hayden halted abruptly and Brent followed suit. "Do you honestly think I don't see what you're doing? You're ridiculously transparent." She poked him hard in the chest with her finger. "You think you can goad me into changing my mind?"

"Well, maybe I've changed my mind, too." His irritation finally showing through, Brent shoved his hands into his pockets. "Had you considered that?"

That brought her up short. No, she hadn't considered that

possibility. Perhaps she'd finally succeeded this afternoon in pushing him away. Exactly what she'd wanted to happen, right? Except the thought of him moving on so quickly make her chest feel heavy and tight. Wanting to hide the emotions she didn't feel capable of keeping off her face, Hayden ducked her head and kept walking. She heard him curse and follow quickly behind her.

"Hayden, wait—"

They both fell silent when they noticed the scene playing out before them. Just ahead, silhouetted by the pink-streaked sunset, their best friend was down on one knee proposing to the other. Only, it wasn't Daniel as they'd expected. Story smiled up at a dumbfounded Daniel from where she knelt on the boardwalk, holding up a ring box.

Hayden couldn't stop the bubble of laughter that rose from her throat. She should have suspected her friend would take convention and knock it on its square ass. At that moment, she couldn't have been more proud of her friend. Over the last two months, she'd transformed into someone who didn't take no for an answer. A woman who made her own decisions and to hell with what anyone else thought. A little blond force to be reckoned with.

It occurred to Hayden then that she herself had turned into quite the opposite. Someone who followed her marching orders, didn't make waves. If she did her duty like a good soldier and married Stuart, she'd never experience the kind of romantic bliss currently radiating from Daniel and Story. She'd never be loved. Would never love anyone back.

Her self-pity didn't belong there, not when the person she treasured most in the world was experiencing her perfect moment in the sun. She hated herself for having that feeling. Hated her impossible situation. Hated the man next to her for making her feel things she might go the rest of her life without ever feeling again.

Hayden felt Brent watching her and turned. Somehow he managed to look as troubled as she felt. She felt moisture coating her cheeks and a jolt of surprise passed through her. When was the last time she'd cried? Her sophomore year of high school. She'd been laid up in bed after having her tonsils removed, woozy from painkillers. *Beaches* had come on and she hadn't been able to find the remote control to change the channel.

Brent reached a hand out to swipe her tears away, but she jerked out of his reach. Fist clenched in midair, his Adam's apple bobbed in his throat. She could tell from his expression that he knew her tears weren't of the happy variety. "Hey. What's going on with you?"

"N-nothing." She swiped impatiently at her tears. "I was…I was just thinking about that movie *Beaches*."

A single eyebrow rose. "That had to be the last thing I expected you to say." He looked thoughtful. "Well, maybe not the last. If you'd said something about the Mets' batting order, I might have fainted." When she didn't respond to his attempt at levity, he sighed, but thankfully he didn't press, nor did he look at her with anything resembling judgment. "Why don't you go back to the hotel? I'll…tell them you went to find your camera."

"Thank you," Hayden managed, before taking off in the opposite direction from which they'd been walking, feeling Brent's gaze on her back as she went. She was thankful for the reprieve. In her current state of mind, she'd only tarnish her friends' happy moment.

Her intention had been to return to her room. Experience her first cry in a decade with a pillow pressed to her face. Instead, she found herself veering into the first bar she passed upon entering the casino. Before she'd even settled onto the barstool, she'd signaled the bartender.

"Tequila, please."

Chapter Thirteen

Brent paced the hallway outside Hayden's room, trying to hold on to his patience. After congratulating Story and Daniel, who'd been too enamored with each other to do anything but acknowledge him with a smile, he'd gone in search of Hayden. Obviously, he'd tried her room first. Then he'd checked the pool and every chick-themed store in the place. Explaining his bigfoot-sized presence in Bath & Body Works had been a real scream.

Why had he let her go off by herself, clearly distraught? He'd watched her standing there in the waning sun, tears streaming down her cheeks, her beauty and vulnerability knocking the breath out of him. Then it all changed. Her features clouded, her shoulders sagged. If his ill-advised comment just seconds before did that to her, he'd kick his own ass. He'd said it expecting her to come right back at him with a rejoinder as she always did, yet she'd abandoned the fight. She must know he didn't mean it. Jesus, wasn't it obvious how badly he wanted her? He could no more change his mind about her than he could fit into a child-sized leotard.

He heard the elevator *ping* and hoped like hell it was Hayden inside. Instead, two thirty-something women got off. Stumbling around a little, they were clearly tipsy. They both came up short when they saw him, bursting out laughing when one got brave and sent him an exaggerated wink. Brent sighed. Then it dawned on him where Hayden would have gone. Good thing he wasn't a detective like Troy or the streets would be overrun with criminals.

Before the elevator could close, he stuck his hand in between the doors to stop their progress and got on, impatiently pressing the lobby button. He started with the bar closest to where he'd seen her re-enter on the casino level. Gypsy Bar. Blaring music and laughter greeted him when he walked inside. When the doorman asked for his ID, Brent gave him a look that said *seriously man?* And kept walking.

He checked the bar area first, not finding her there. Early on a Saturday night, the room hadn't yet filled to capacity, but was still reasonably busy. Several customers were already dancing, Brent noticed. Then he did a double take. Hayden, drink in hand, danced in the middle of a large group like her life depended on it. Arms in the air, hips twisting. He'd never seen her look so uninhibited apart from their one night together when she'd transformed before his very eyes. As Brent moved closer, he saw that her skin was rosy and slightly dewy from exertion, the blue dress clinging to her curves as she moved her hips to the rhythm. Her hair had finally given up its battle with perfection, curling at the ends, a dark wave coming down to obscure half her face. She looked how he imagined she would if he ever got her into bed again. Without a time limit or any ridiculous rules. He got hard thinking about it. Watching her dip and sway, he imagined her on top of him instead, riding out her orgasm with the use of his body.

If you stand here ogling her like a jackass any longer, you'll embarrass yourself. Not to mention, he wasn't the only male who'd taken notice of Hayden. When one such guy elbowed his buddy and nodded in Hayden's direction, Brent's feet were moving purposefully toward her before he'd even made a conscious decision. When he got within five feet, she looked up as if she'd sensed him. Heat thrummed low in his belly when he got a close look at her. Perfectly polished Hayden made him hot, but *this* girl...fuck, she burned him from the inside.

She'd always accused him of being a caveman. Right now, he could freely admit she'd been right. A furious, pounding need began inside him. Something about her lost expression, her defenselessness, called to that deeply primal part of him. The one that demanded he throw her over his shoulder and take her home so he could pleasure her, see to her needs, until she fell asleep and forgot why she'd been troubled in the first place. When she woke up again, he'd be inside her. Between thrusts, he'd gladly inform her that her man had taken care of her problems, just like he always would. Then he'd fuck her back to sleep.

Eyes scanning his face, her lips parted just slightly, telling him he'd done a poor job of hiding his inner thoughts. He didn't care. The caveman was rearing its head, urging him to rip off his shirt and let her look her fill. Let her see who'd come to take her to bed. The protector in him demanded answers. Demanded he find out why she'd been crying. Find out what could possibly put that forlorn expression on her face, distress her to the point she felt compelled to act out this way. So unlike her usual self.

He sensed, however, that an interrogation was the last thing she needed. So doing his best to tame the caveman, he opened his arms, relieved when she simply walked into them. She stood on her tiptoes to wrap her arms around his neck, stretching her body flush against his, and he held her, swaying them on the dance floor.

After a few minutes of silence between them, she spoke haltingly next to his ear. "I'm so happy for Daniel and Story, you know. *So* happy. I just..." Her fingers slid into his hair and his eyes shut. Brent could hear the ever-so-slight running together of her words and put her at about four drinks. Not drunk exactly, but her decisions would be influenced. He needed to remember that. "But it must be amazing, you know? Getting exactly what you always wanted. Having so much...control of your future."

Brent frowned against her head. If anything, a girl like Hayden, money and influence coming out of her ears, got any damn thing she wanted. He focused on the second half of what she said instead. "Who's got you feeling out of control, duchess?"

Hayden shook her head, knocking against his chin in a way he found so endearing, his throat hurt.

"Tell me so I can set them straight."

She looked up at him then, all traces of vulnerability gone. He recognized that look. She'd worn it the night she cuffed him and slowly stripped herself of clothes, and him of his sanity. She wanted to distract him from his questions and...*shit*. It worked. As her attention snagged on his mouth, her body slid down low, pressing firmly into his on the way back up. He couldn't stop himself from tilting his hips so she could feel what she'd done to him. Her fingers traced over his shoulders and down his chest, undoing the top button of his shirt, then she kissed the exposed flesh. She traced a path with her lips up his neck and over his chin, ending where their mouths met. Brent kissed her hungrily, starved for the taste of her, his inner caveman pounding his chest again as he claimed her as his own in the middle of the dance floor. When she moaned in her throat and shuddered, he reluctantly pulled away.

"I'm still pissed at you," Hayden said, head pressed to his

chest.

"Everyone's always pissed at me. It's just part of my charm." He released his own unsteady breath as Hayden laughed. How he could make a joke when he felt so painfully turned-on his knees might give out at any moment, Brent had no clue. She'd *needed* to laugh, that's why. It was fast becoming obvious that he'd put himself through a dozen varieties of torture to give her what she needed. When had that started? Why didn't he want it to end?

"So you didn't really change your mind, then? You still…?"

Brent tipped her chin up. "Hayden, look at me. I'm dancing. You think I'd dance for a girl unless I wanted her like crazy?" He ran his thumb across her bottom lip, groaning when her tongue darted out to lick him. "I guess you haven't figured it out yet, huh? This week alone, I let you cuff me, stuff me into a suit, and inflict me with Blue-Ball Syndrome."

Her lips quirked up. "Is that an actual medical diagnosis?"

"Yeah. It is now," he growled. "They're naming it after me, too. 'I got a case of the Brents.' People will be saying that for centuries to come."

Hayden's eyes narrowed. "Wait, you said 'I *let* you cuff me'?"

He winked at her. When she sputtered in disbelief, he cut her off with a kiss. She sagged into him almost immediately, actually managing to knock him back a step. He caught her around the waist with his arm. "Hey, how much have you had to drink?"

• • •

Hayden bit her lip and looked up at Brent with mock innocence. He looked all noble and protective standing there, waiting for her answer, a concerned frown marring his forehead. It made her want to climb up his body and whisper very bad things in his ear until he cracked. She might have a few drinks buzzing through her brain, but wanting Brent naked wasn't a product of her over-imbibing. Before she'd even set foot in the bar she'd wanted that, so she wasn't about to let him get away with this whole honorable-policeman act. Not by a long shot.

One *teeny* little product of her loosened inhibitions was her sudden determination that she needed one more hot, tear-up-the-sheets night with Brent. If she agreed to consign herself to a lifetime as a trophy wife, she wanted to experience his brand of passion one more time. So she could tuck it deep into her memory bank and call on it whenever needed. The part of her brain hanging on to the cliff's edge of sobriety warned her this was a bad decision, but she tuned it out. She needed him so bad, her body ached. Her breasts, her hands, the flesh between her thighs all begged for contact with him. He'd know what she needed, even if she herself didn't know right then. Just knew that Brent would give it to her.

"I've had three drinks."

He grunted. "More like five."

She tried again. "How about four?"

"We're not bargaining here, woman."

Excited by the challenge, Hayden slid her hands up the front of his shirt, satisfied when the muscles bunched under her hands. *All that power. Mine. Just for tonight.*

Using his shoulders for leverage, she leaned up to whisper in his ear. "Brent, take me somewhere private. Where I can wrap my legs around all that muscle. Somewhere you can take off my teeny, tiny panties and fuck me hard."

"*Jesus Christ*," he moaned. As if acting on their own, his hands dropped to her ass and hauled her up against him. Hayden whimpered when she felt his enormous erection probing her through the thin material of her dress. "Are you out of your goddamn mind saying something like that to me in public? It's all I can do right now not to bend you over the nearest table and fuck you senseless with everyone watching. Maybe it would teach you to be more careful with that mouth."

Hot, wet heat flooded her, spreading between her legs. She almost had him...just one more push. "My mouth knows exactly how—"

Before the words were fully spoken, Brent began dragging her across the dance floor, scanning the bar as he went. Apparently satisfied that no one paid them any attention, he pushed through a door with an exit sign above it and pulled her behind him into a dark, empty hallway. The only light illuminating the corridor emanated from two exit signs on either end. Music, muffled now, pounded through the door, mingling with their panting breaths.

"On your knees."

Combined with the thumping bass, the erratic rhythm of her heart beat loudly in her ears. Every cell in her body hummed in needy anticipation. She fell to her knees without a single hesitation, desperate to wring every drop of pleasure from tonight. Not just her own, but Brent's as well. Their hands met in a tangle as they worked frantically to unbuckle his belt and lower the zipper of his dress pants. She devoured the sight of his erection, the evidence of how badly he wanted her.

He braced one hand above her on the wall; the other gripped her head and urged her forward. At the last second, just before her mouth made contact, he pulled her hair to stop her. When he spoke, his voice sounded raw and dark. "Uh-uh. First, you finish what you were going to say. Your mouth knows exactly how—what?"

Hayden's breath raced in and out as she looked up at him from her position on the floor. He towered over her, his strength making her feel so fragile. Yet at the same time, she knew she held the reins. Her mouth, her body, represented his pleasure and they both knew it. If possible, the realization heated her even more. It made pretending the opposite twice as heady. She gripped the base of his erection in her fist. "My mouth knows exactly how you like it."

"Keep going," he ordered. "Be very specific or I'll make you wait an hour for a ride."

She flicked out her tongue and caught the tip, making Brent groan. "You like me to take it deep. As deep as I can. You like when I suck hard on the tip."

"That's right. Now, open your mouth and make it count. I earned it." No sooner had she obeyed his harsh command than he guided himself between her damp, parted lips. She moaned at the smooth feel of him on her tongue even as she struggled to wrap her mouth around him completely. Unlike last time, she didn't tease him. She'd have been teasing herself in the process, because every taste, every groan she wrung from his throat, was like an aphrodisiac straight to her brain. Her hand stroked his girth in time with her mouth, faster and faster until she felt him start to shake, and exulted in his loss of composure.

"Stop, baby. Now. Oh God, please stop." Ignoring his request, she swirled her tongue around the tip, then sucked it hard enough to hollow her cheeks. Distantly, she heard his fist connect with the concrete wall, then he was dragging her to her feet. He pushed her back against the cool, hard surface and reached a hand beneath her dress to yank down her panties. All the while, she watched his flushed face, exulting in the desperation she saw there.

As frantic as Brent was to get inside her, as badly as she needed to give him relief, Hayden felt the now-familiar desire for control tingling in her limbs. She'd been spinning out of control all week, maybe her whole life, if she was honest with herself. Everyone else saw the coolly self-possessed Hayden, but truthfully, she followed the dictates of others, the stuffy world she lived in. The urge to make her own rules beckoned to her. Brent would do whatever she asked of him. If she told him to stop right now, he would, even if it killed him. While she didn't want to abuse that honorable part of him, she couldn't deny the irresistible need to test it.

"Spread your thighs wide for me. I'm gonna fuck you until my next thrust is the only thing keeping you sane." He boosted her effortlessly up against the wall so she could wrap her legs around his waist. She felt him, hot and thick at her entrance, as he rolled on a condom. Then he filled her in one, hard shove that nearly pushed her over the edge. Their sharp cries echoed in the empty hallway.

"Don't move." Her words came out in a whispered rush, entirely of their own accord. "No moving until I say you can."

Brent stilled, buried deep inside her. Their eyes met and the agony she saw in his almost forced her to give in, but she couldn't deny the surge of undiluted pleasure. Having this big, robust man obey her was pure decadence. God, she needed this. How could she live without this?

"Hayden." Teeth clenched, his voice shook. "Please let me move, baby. I can only take so much. I'm…" He released a shuddering groan when she clenched him with her inner muscles. "I'm worried…if you play this game with me much longer…I could hurt you when you finally let me… Fuck, I'm dying. This is the end, right?"

She tugged down the top of her dress, her hand clumsy. "Taste me first."

His mouth descended on her breasts with a growl, frantically licking and sucking her nipples. Hayden's head fell back on her shoulders, pure hedonistic bliss spearing through her system. Impaled on his pulsing erection, all but pinned to the wall while he devoured her breasts, could only be described as the most erotic experience of her life. And she had the privilege of calling the shots. Nothing compared to this lust-drunk feeling. Nothing ever would. An earth-shattering climax loomed, but she wanted to prolong this moment.

She grabbed a fistful of his hair and pulled his head away from her breasts. His eyes were feverish, glazed with need. It nearly sent her spiraling into release, but she held it back.

"Please," he whispered roughly. "Please."

She spoke through panting breaths. "Tell me what you're going to do to me first."

Brent buried his face against her neck and moaned. She reveled in the desperate sound. Between her thighs, his body shook like it might implode at any moment. Raw power. Leashed. By her.

"I'm going to cram your tight pussy full over and over again," he growled. "I'm going to fuck you until your ears ring. I'm going to bite you hard. Mark you. Ruin you."

Hayden's orgasm slammed through her, turning her inside out. She barely had the breath in her body to tell him to move, but she somehow managed it through the waves of incredible heat. "Now, Brent. *Now.*"

The last coherent thought in Hayden's head evaporated as Brent unleashed himself on her. He hooked his arms under her knees and shoved her thighs wide with enough force to make her gasp. Then the pounding began. He held nothing back, slamming into her without an ounce of mercy, grinding her back into the wall with the force of his thrusts. The slapping of flesh combined with Brent's animalistic grunts into her neck undid her. She heard herself calling his name, her voice sounding unfamiliar to her ears. Her nails dug into the taut flesh of his brawny shoulders, her hips undulated into his unyielding drives.

"Is this what you wanted, duchess? A punishment fuck?"

His teeth sank into her shoulder with a growl. "It works both ways. You punish me, I'll punish you right back."

Like last time, his coarse speech sent her to the brink of orgasm. She hastened toward it, powerless to do anything but experience the glorious pleasure. "*Yes*, Brent. Punish me. Show me what I did to you."

Eyes lit with challenge, he jerked her off the wall. Supporting her with strong hands that gripped her bottom, he worked her up and down his rigid erection, the new position creating a slippery friction against her clitoris. With a throaty moan, she clutched his shoulders and leaned back, pumping her hips in time with his. They watched each other through the haze of lust, Brent's sexually charged gaze hurtling her into orgasm. She struggled to keep her eyes open so she could watch him find his own release and was rewarded by his expression of absolute surrender. His teeth sank into his bottom lip, but it did nothing to mute the roar of gratification that escaped him.

No sooner had he finished than he let Hayden slide down his body to the floor. Before she could decipher his intention, he spun her toward the wall. Her palms pressed against the cool surface to brace herself as his big hand came down hard once on her bottom with a loud *slap* that echoed through the empty hallway, sending a wave of ecstasy through her. Then he pulled her back against his chest and held her close, breath rasping in her hair.

She didn't have the strength to question him. If he wasn't holding her up at that moment, she suspected she'd be in a boneless heap on the floor. Perhaps it didn't *require* any examination. He'd accepted her needs without question. Allowed her to discover this new part of herself, all but abusing him in the process. She could do the same for him. And dammit, hadn't she loved it? The sting of his hand, knowing she'd pushed him to his breaking point? Yes, she had.

Turned away from Brent, with him unable to see her face, she felt the sudden need to reassure herself about her actions. He'd been in pain. She'd…been turned on by his torment. She didn't know how to feel about that. "I, um…I'm sorry I made you wait like that."

"Duchess, you can mistreat me like that any day of the week," he murmured, obviously still recovering. When she didn't say anything for a long stretch, he turned her around to study her face. She had no idea what he saw there. Didn't even know *herself* at that moment. "Hey. Look at me." She complied. "I'm a big, bad dude. I can take it. And Hayden?" He kissed her long and hard. "Let's get on the same page. I'm the only one who has the privilege of taking it ever again."

Chapter Fourteen

Brent glanced over at a silent Hayden as they walked down the deserted boardwalk. Well past sundown, the crowds had descended on the casinos and nightclubs, the beach forgotten until the next day. Crashing waves combined with distant cheers from inside the casino walls. Flashing lights from the gambling establishments pulsed, creating an ambiance specific to Atlantic City. He noticed a light breeze lift Hayden's hair and mentally shook himself. If he'd started noticing things like breeze and ambiance, he was in bigger trouble than he thought.

It didn't help that Hayden had gone mostly silent after his declaration that he intended to be the only one on whom she inflicted her particular brand of torture from now on. Hell, he'd made that decision before tonight, but no need to vocalize that fact. If her reaction served as any indication, it wouldn't exactly have her floating on air and singing show tunes. Apparently it was going to take some convincing that they could work. Yes, they'd started off as adversaries. Yes, they came from two completely different worlds. And, oh yes, they were as different as two people could get. Seeing each other exclusively would mean an open mind on both their parts. A lot of compromise. A shit-ton of arguing. But holy hell, if it ended the way tonight had, he'd deal with just about anything she could throw at him.

Even now, he craved her body like an addiction. It had begun almost immediately, the relentless ache to get back between her thighs. See how far she'd push him next time. He'd never been driven so far outside of his own consciousness as he'd been with his cock tucked tightly inside of her. He'd never considered himself someone who enjoyed delayed gratification. Now? *Delayed gratification, party of one. Your table is ready.* Christ, he'd come like a speeding freight train. It had felt so damn unbelievable that it almost hurt. What happened afterward, the spanking…well, he didn't really have an explanation for that, except that he'd wanted to punish her for making him feel so incredible. Where was the logic in that?

Logic didn't apply to them, he supposed. They'd been two opposite magnets that suddenly switched poles and were now compelled toward the other. When it came to their physical connection, the differences between them didn't matter. They only heightened the experience. If he applied logic to their situation, he'd probably conclude that they were wrong for each other and the ridiculous sex was a product of months of foreplay. That's what the fighting had been. He recognized that now. He'd been goading her toward his bed since day one and thank Christ it had finally worked. Otherwise, he'd be missing out on the best sex of his ever-loving life.

So, enjoy the sex and keep it simple, right? No messy commitments…right? Yet the thought of limiting their relationship to a physical diversion made him all kinds of antsy. He didn't want to limit them. He wanted to hear her say the words, that she was *his*. His to fight with. His to soothe.

His to fuck. No one else's. Hayden, however, didn't appear to share his interest in the idea. Good thing he never turned down a challenge. Especially when she looked like some kind of mussed-up sex kitten in her clingy dress, hair tangling around her thoughtful face, lips swollen from his treatment of them, from their unbelievable treatment of his cock.

Brent released a slow breath. One battle at a time. *Get her talking, ease the tension you created by speaking too soon, jackass, and* then *worry about getting her back into bed.*

"So…*Beaches*, huh?" Brent cleared his throat. "What is that, some kind of chick flick?" Of course, he'd seen *Beaches*. Bette Midler was a national treasure. He'd keep that to himself though, in the interest of her not questioning his masculinity.

A brief flicker of humor shone in her eyes before she hid it. "No, it's a buddy cop movie. You would love it. Action-packed. Definitely no singing."

Brent nodded, pretending to take her seriously. "I'll add it to my Netflix queue." Unable to help himself, he took her hand. "And if you come over and watch it with me, I promise not to sing along to 'Wind Beneath My Wings.'"

Her momentary pause over his impulsive hand-holding turned into surprised laugher. The kind that made his chest tighten. "You're so lucky your boys weren't here to hear that."

"Who do you think performs duets with me?"

She pursed her lips. "Normally I would say Daniel, but Matt could be a potential dark horse."

Kind of like him and Hayden. For so long, they thought they had each other pegged, but it turned out they hadn't even scratched the surface. She'd never seen it coming. "So *Beaches*…a classic piece of cinema, but a weird thing to think about while witnessing a marriage proposal."

She glanced sideways at him, then sighed. "I guess I was trying to remember the last time I cried."

Brent held his breath, afraid he'd open his mouth and some boneheaded comment would emerge, ruining this rare glimpse under her surface.

"I'd just gotten my tonsils taken out and I was too doped up to get out of bed and find the remote," she said. "*Beaches* came on. Complete with commercial interruptions. I was helpless to escape it."

Brent laughed. "How old were you?"

"Fifteen."

He pulled her to a stop. "You haven't cried in a decade?" She looked uncomfortable and he wanted to take back his shocked question. "Wait. What about chopping onions? That counts."

Her mouth relaxed into a smile. "Then I guess it's only been a few weeks. Bette Midler and onions are my Kryptonite. What's yours?"

I think it might be you. He swallowed. "Sports movies. When the underdog comes back after halftime to win. I can't keep it together during the coach's obligatory halftime speech and then it's a rapid decline into wuss-hood." He thought for a moment. "Also, brownies. My mother's, specifically."

"Brownies."

He nodded once. "Don't judge me until you've had one."

They walked for a while after that, until he pulled her to a stop at the wooden rail so they could watch the ocean, illuminated by the neon signs behind them. Their arms touched and he barely resisted the urge to pull her close. Too much too soon. "What's it like having your parents in the same neighborhood?" he asked instead.

"Exhausting."

Brent watched as she turned serious, then considered him closely for a moment as though she couldn't decide why she'd suddenly decided to be honest with him. He couldn't decide either. Only knew he wanted her to keep going.

"They're my parents, they've done everything for me. But...it's complicated."

Silently, he waited for her to say more. When she didn't, he prodded her. "Talk to me, Hayden."

She rubbed her arms, the breeze having turned cold. Brent gave in to his impulse and pulled her into his arms, resting his chin on top of her head. He couldn't ignore the way they fit together. How right it felt. "My father, the man you charmed so effortlessly the other night, is actually my uncle. My father died when I was young, leaving me with my mother. She was young, far too young for a child, and they'd never bothered to get married. So my uncle took us in." She laughed into his chest. "I have no idea why I'm telling you this."

"I don't either," he said, hiding his shock over her revelation. "But I'm glad you are."

"Okay. That's good enough for me." Slowly, her arms went around his waist. Brent closed his eyes against the foreign emotions bubbling in his chest. He sensed Hayden wanted to say more so once again, he reined in his need to fill the silence with whatever nonsense popped into his head. "He didn't have to take us in. I kind of owe him for everything, you know? Even if sometimes it means I have to do things that are...difficult."

Brent looked down at the top of her head, confused by her cryptic tone. He had the overwhelming feeling that she was trying to tell him something, but he couldn't decipher it. *Don't push too hard or she'll shut down.* Still, he needed to say what was on his mind. "You don't owe him. Look what he got out of the deal. A beautiful daughter who runs around making everyone else happy. If you ask me, he owes you."

She stilled in his arms, looking up at him after a moment. "I wish it worked that way. It's not always that simple."

"Yes, it is." He couldn't account for the frisson of panic

over the finality of her tone. *What am I missing?* "I say it is that easy for someone like you. And I'm not talking about the money. I'm talking about you."

After a moment of staring up into his face thoughtfully, she brightened, although he could tell it took an effort on her part. "So...two jobs. One that includes the dismantling and rigging of explosives. A mortgage. Your sister's college tuition. Supporting your brother's family. I say you don't know the first thing about easy, Mr. Mason."

Oh boy, he liked her calling him that. Brent stiffened behind his fly. *Ignore it. You're having an actual meaningful conversation with her.* He also couldn't deny a flare of pleasure that she recognized his hard work. He'd never needed the recognition before, but his inner caveman had decided to make another appearance. *That's right, I take care of what's mine. I'll take care of you, too. Let me. Oh God, let me.*

He kicked the caveman in the nuts and refocused on her. Downplayed his situation like he always did. "Yeah. Well, my brother will be home soon from overseas...and Lucy, she won't be in college forever. The mechanic gig is temporary."

"Don't make light of it." Hayden shook her head. "I'm sorry I ever did."

"An apology from the duchess? Now who's going soft?"

She bit her lip and ran her hands down his chest. He promptly forgot what he'd been saying. "I'll tell you a secret in addition to my apology. That day at the garage...I would have let you have me on that desk. It would have taken very little effort. You came out looking so"—her nails scraped over his nipples—"rugged. I wanted to rip those coveralls off of you."

"What did I tell you about speaking to me this way in public?"

When she laughed, he knew he didn't quite pull off his warning tone. "So? What are you going to do about it?"

He growled low in his throat. "If you pretend for even a second that you're not staying in my room tonight, there's going to be trouble in Atlantic City."

"Ooh. I like trouble."

Before the words were completely out of her mouth, Brent hauled her over his shoulder. Hayden gasped, then couldn't stop laughing as they walked down the empty boardwalk.

"You want trouble?" He smacked her ass. "You've got it, duchess."

Chapter Fifteen

Hayden peeked out from under heavy eyelids, head still fuzzy from sleep. It took her mere seconds to remember the night before and where she'd fallen asleep. After all, she didn't often wake up with two hundred and fifty pounds of solid, naked male wrapped around her. Brent's arm was slung over her waist, anchoring her against his chest, preventing any movement. Her legs were trapped in between his heavier ones. She could feel his soft exhalations ruffling the hair on top of her head, but surprisingly, he didn't snore. She'd have guessed he would snore like a grizzly bear.

It took her a moment to realize a huge smile had spread across her face. She was glad he'd trapped her in his muscle-man fortress, because she didn't want to move. Didn't want to leave the bed in which they'd spent the night, making love for hours on end. He'd brought her to orgasm so many times she'd have to use her permanently curled toes to help count. She'd done the same for him. Teasing, tasting, torturing, until he reached his breaking point. They'd hid nothing from each other, reveling in weaknesses and strengths. Differences and similarities.

Last night would stand out in her memory for two reasons. One, as the night she'd been pleasured so thoroughly, she'd partially lost her voice from screaming. Second, as the night she realized she could never marry Stuart. She had no idea what lay between her and Brent, but she knew giving up this feeling wasn't an option. She'd just discovered this entirely new side of herself and she needed to explore it. And by some strange miracle of nature, she could only imagine exploring it with Brent—someone who, up until a week ago, she'd despised with every fiber of her being. Someone she had practically nothing in common with. Yet as she lay snuggled against his body, she found herself looking forward to him waking up. Talking to him. And, oh yes, she could already feel that delicious tightening in her belly, the tickle between her thighs. He would know what to do. How to satisfy her.

A tinge of guilt sparked in her chest. The last thing she should be thinking about was sex. Later on today, she would need to break the news to her parents that she wouldn't, *couldn't,* marry Stuart. That everything her father had worked for would turn to dust because she couldn't fathom a life spent married to someone she didn't love. That she'd finally realized she was capable of doing more with her life, starting with her charity. Of course, her mother wouldn't understand. She'd call Hayden selfish. Perhaps she'd be right. But it didn't change her decision. Until now, her sole purpose in life had been to make her father happy, repay him for taking her in as a child. She simply couldn't do it anymore. Her life, her happiness, was simply too large a sacrifice.

Had her feelings for Brent made the decision for her? The thought troubled Hayden. He'd undoubtedly played a major role, but the newfound connection between them was still so fresh. Turning down an offer of marriage from Stuart to take a chance on the unknown might not be her wisest move. Still, the idea of exploring this fragile new relationship pulled her. If fighting and sleeping together could actually be termed a *relationship*, as opposed to *insanity*.

Her chaotic thoughts were interrupted by a surge of heat as Brent's hand snaked over her hip to disappear between her thighs. Immediately, her entire body went on alert, skin tingling, breath catching in her lungs. He removed the big leg pinning her thighs down and opened her to his skilled fingers, stroking the damp flesh in between. Against her bottom, his erection swelled and she circled her hips. When he growled next to her ear, she shuddered.

"Next time you need me, wake me up." He bit her earlobe, tugged. "You don't spend a minute unsatisfied in my bed. Understand?"

"Yes, I understand." She gasped when he rubbed her clitoris with the pad of his thumb. After last night, her flesh felt extremely sensitive to his touch, almost as though she hovered on the brink of release, her body anticipating the way it would inevitably shatter under his attention. She tipped her head back, seeking his mouth, and was rewarded by a long, hot, possessive kiss. By the time it ended, she writhed against him mindlessly.

"Where did we leave off last night?" He pushed his middle finger deep, stroking the spot he'd used to exploit her desperation just hours before. "Whose turn was it to be in charge?"

"Y-yours."

"Good, because I can practically hear the wheels turning in that stubborn head of yours." He added another finger, pushed tight, and held until she whimpered. "You listen best when I'm buried in that sweet pussy. Get on your stomach. I'm about to clear up any misunderstandings."

Practically shaking with lust, Hayden did as he asked. He slipped his fingers free to shove a pillow beneath her hips, putting her in a provocative position, face pressed against the mattress, bottom in the air. "What misunderstandings?"

He fisted her hair and tugged. "Who's in charge here?"

She sucked in a breath. "You are."

"Right. Don't rush me." He reached across her body to the bedside table and retrieved a condom from the jumbo pack they'd bought last night. She heard him rip the foil and roll on their protection. "You'll have no more questions when I'm finished."

She felt his mouth at the backs of her knees, kissing and biting her flesh. His mouth moved higher, up her thighs, over her buttocks. He lingered there, biting extra hard just underneath the base of her spine. It sent a shiver of anticipation coursing through her body, heat prickling her nerve endings. When his lips continued their path up her back, his big hands squeezed and kneaded her backside with punishing fingers. Finally his lips reached her neck and he slid his hands up her sides and around to her breasts. At the same time, he worked himself against her upturned bottom, grinding her hips down into the pillow.

"Part your legs just a little for me." She did as he asked. "Good girl. Now push your fine ass even higher. *Higher.* That's it. Right there." He shoved into her with a groan. Hayden echoed the sound into the mattress. "Straighten your legs now. Lock me in."

When Brent pulled out and drove back into her, sensation rocketed through her system. Something about the angle, the position, the smooth, slick thrusts, made her crazy with need. She wanted to scream at him to go faster, harder, but she held her tongue. To make up for her silence, she milked him with her inner walls, squeezing him inside her. The harder he had to work to thrust into her slight opening, the wilder he became. His rhythm increased along with the intensity of his surges until Hayden was forced to hold on to the wrought iron headboard.

Brent gathered her hair in his fist and pulled her head back. When he spoke, his voice sounded raw and severe. "I'm going to ask you some questions now. The answer to *all* of them is my name. You following me?"

She made a breathy sound of agreement, but apparently unsatisfied with her answer, he tugged on his fistful of her hair. "Yes. *Yes!*"

He filled her completely and held his hips still. "Who gets the deepest, Hayden?"

"Brent," she moaned.

Two quick thrusts. "Who gets fucking hot when his naughty little bad girl makes him work hard for it? Makes him wait?"

Oh God, that nearly sent her hurtling over the edge. Her muscles clenched, her thighs shook. Any minute now. "Brent!"

"Who tongued your pussy for an hour straight last night?"

"Brent," she sobbed. "Brent."

He let go of her hair and buried his face in her neck, voice dropping considerably. "Who do you belong to?"

His name sat right on the tip of her tongue. Her instincts told her to scream it. When she didn't answer right away, she felt him tense on top of her. Her silence was hurting him. Hating his pain, loving the sense of rightness her heart's answer made her feel, she threw caution to the wind and followed her instincts. "*Brent.*"

On top of her, his body shuddered. "Hayden," he groaned into her neck. Then he gripped her hips and began to move once again, his powerful drives quickly casting her into oblivion. She had no time to prepare for the release that tore her apart, feelings too close to the surface to keep them separate from her physical pleasure. They overwhelmed her, threatened to sink her, but Brent's presence, his steady voice, managed to anchor her.

As always, when he climaxed, Hayden marveled at the contrast of uncommon strength and powerlessness in him. He could do nothing but ride out the ecstasy, a slave to his body's needs. *Her* body's needs. She closed her eyes and memorized the shaking of his body, the choked noises he couldn't contain. The way he held on to her as if she, too, had somehow become his anchor when neither of them expected it.

He lay down on the bed beside her, sweat dotting his forehead. She didn't hesitate, but went straight into his arms, sighing when he planted a kiss on her head.

After a moment, he broke the silence. "Did that answer all of your questions?"

She smiled into his chest. "Nope. Still wondering what we're having for breakfast." Laughter rumbled through him, but he waited for her real answer. She took a silent breath. "Yes. Although if you want to remind me that same way whenever possible, I'd appreciate it."

...

Brent shoved yesterday's clothes into his overnight bag, throwing another impatient glance at the door connecting his room to Hayden's. Christ, she'd gone to shower and change a mere half hour ago and he already missed the sight of her. He'd rushed through his shower, hoping she'd do the same so they could spend the remaining hour before checkout together, but he'd emerged from the shower to find her door locked. He knew her game now and it only excited him. It was her turn to run the show. She wanted to frustrate him, make him wait. Perhaps she'd wait until they had ten minutes to go before coming to him so he'd have to take her quickly. Frantically.

He stared hard at the door, contemplating the idea of knocking. Saying something dirty to her through the barrier, giving her no choice but to open it. She'd be soft and fragrant from her shower. Her scent still lingered in the room, but he needed it up close. He didn't have a name for her scent. Expensive, appetizing, light, tempting.

Shit. Why don't you just grab some hotel stationery and write a quick haiku, Romeo? Ode to Hayden's body. While his fevered thoughts regarding her body could easily take up eight hotel notepads, he could completely double that on Hayden the sensual flirt. Hayden the rumpled jokester. Hayden the girl who carried around hidden pain, locking it up so tight she rarely allowed anyone a glimpse. She'd given him a brief glance last night on the boardwalk and now he wanted more. To learn every part of her. Find out more about what made her tick.

Furthermore, Brent wanted to show her the parts of himself he normally kept hidden under his loud, abrasive personality. The one he showed the world, but didn't necessarily sum him up. He wanted her to see more. Wanted to *show* her more.

To his relief, she'd agreed in her own roundabout way to give him that chance. All right, his methods for gaining her agreement hadn't exactly been fair, but when had they ever fought fair? He and Hayden did things their own unusual way and he wouldn't change it for anything. They'd have bumps along the way to finding out where this relationship would go, but dammit if he didn't look forward to arguing. And hell... making up? He got hard just thinking about it.

His cell phone rang beside him on the bed. His sister Lucy's picture popped up on the screen and he shivered in horror at having a hard-on at the same time. He shook his head to dispel thoughts of an angry yet turned-on Hayden from his mind and answered the phone.

"Luce. What's wrong? You need bail money again?"

"Funny. You should take your act on the road." He couldn't help but smile at her sarcastic response. His sister looked and acted like a sorority girl, but she was hell on wheels. Yet underneath her strawberry curls, so like their mother's, lurked a closet brainiac. Her intelligence motivated him to work twice as many hours. What was a couple extra hours in a greasy garage when his little sister might take her college education and change the world someday? If she didn't get herself killed skydiving or speeding on her moped first. "Besides, that one time was a misunderstanding. I didn't know bonfires weren't allowed on campus. There should be clearly marked signs."

"That say what? 'Use your common sense'?"

She snorted. "All right, I'm going to let you get away with that one. I'm too happy with you today to take issue with your stuffy tone."

He glanced back at the connecting door. What the hell was taking Hayden so long? "Happy with me?"

"Of course! How come you didn't tell me you were applying for tuition grants? I would have helped fill out paperwork. Who knew I was even eligible for one?"

Brent felt a sense of foreboding settle in his stomach. His sixth sense kicked into high gear. This was somehow bad news. He just knew it. "Okay, let's start from the beginning. What grant are you talking about? Who told you the tuition had been paid?"

"The bursar called me. They received funds for the remainder of my tuition from the…" She trailed off and he heard some papers rustling in the background. "The Winstead Foundation."

His hand tightened on the phone until he heard the plastic creak in his fist. When he spoke, the words felt like they were being strangled from his throat. "Did they say anything else?"

"Nope. Just that I'd been personally selected by the head of the foundation. Some rich person named Hayden Winstead. I'm not even sure if that's a man or a woman's name. What do you think?"

"Woman," he answered through clenched teeth. "She's a woman."

A long pause. "O-kay. You seem pretty sure about that."

"Oh, I am. I have to go, Luce." He hung up on her concerned response. For long moments, he sat there staring into space, trying to get his anger under control. Then he realized he didn't want to get it under control. In his life, he couldn't remember ever feeling this way. He didn't have a name for the foreign emotion boiling in his chest. Just knew that in one fell swoop, Hayden had managed to take away everything he'd worked so hard to accomplish. Every day, he got up and busted his ass to provide for his loved ones. It's how he defined himself. How he looked at himself in the mirror. What the hell had been the point if someone who didn't understand the concept of money just made a phone call and took the privilege away from him?

As if on cue, the connecting door opened and Hayden walked in looking so goddamn beautiful it made breathing difficult. She smiled as though she hadn't just turned his world upside down by passing on her American Express number to pay for his sister's education. As if she hadn't just stripped him of the only thing he had. His pride.

"Story called. They want to check out and grab brunch somewhere before heading back. Sound good? Daniel said he'll show up when he's ready, whatever that means." Her easy glide in his direction faltered. "What's wrong?"

"When did you do it?" he said quietly, voice echoing in his own ears. "Did you even consider consulting me first?"

"Do...what?" She shook her head. "I'm not following."

He pushed off the bed, scoffing as he passed her. "My sister just called me. If your plan was to play stupid, you should have made the grant anonymous."

She stared at him for a beat. "You might as well be talking in Swahili. I gather you're upset, but I assure you I'm not playing stupid."

"Right, Hayden. Just keep up the act and maybe the idiot mechanic will eventually buy it." He shoved his wallet and keys into the front pocket of his jeans. "My sister just called. The Winstead Foundation paid for her college tuition. Selected personally by Miss Hayden Winstead herself."

Her face drained completely of color. She opened her mouth to speak but only a few confused words emerged. "I don't...but that makes no...sense."

Even with righteous anger coursing through his veins, the sight of her in distress felt like a hard kick in the stomach. He dismissed his need to yank her into his arms and forgive her, just so she'd smile again. But he wouldn't mean it. So he stood his ground.

"I guess I shouldn't be surprised. You tried to pay me after our last night together." His pronouncement caused her to fall back a step. He ignored the immediate sting of regret over his choice of words. There was no room for regret in addition to his resentment. "I didn't accept your money last time. I won't accept it this time. Or *ever*. Keep your goddamn money, Hayden. We're not all sitting around hoping for a piece of the Winstead fortune."

"Of course not. That's ridiculous. I never saw it like th—"

"God. Can you even see outside of your privileged bubble? Just because your life is planned and controlled down to the smallest detail, doesn't mean you can control everyone else with money, too. What you did was purely selfish."

Brent watched as she absorbed his words. And changed right before his very eyes. In a matter of seconds, she went from the casual, playful girl he'd spent the night with to the cool, ivory-tower-dwelling princess he'd fought with relentlessly for months. Warm, chocolate-brown eyes turned shuttered. Her posture stiffened. Brent wanted to shout at the ceiling as he watched her slip away from him, knowing that whatever they'd found in the darkness last night had just been obliterated. Ironically, instead of defusing the bomb-like situation, he'd allowed it to explode in his face.

Hayden laughed without humor and it sliced through him. "I can't believe I thought for one second that you could get past the damn money. It's never going to end, is it? You think I'm a spoiled brat and no matter what I say or do, nothing will change that. Every time we fight, I'm going to be reminded of how very little I know about the real world, about honest work. You'll do it every time. Well, guess what? I'm already sick of it." She took a step toward the door. "Count me out."

Brent followed her. "You went behind my back. Accomplished something in minutes that should've taken me years. You really can't understand why that would fucking bother me?"

"I understand that it bothers you, Brent. I understand," she returned. "But without giving me a chance to say a word, you went right to your knee-jerk response of *crucify the rich girl.*"

He shrugged. "If the Italian leather pump fits..."

Fuck. That one finally pushed her too far. He briefly considered hiding underneath the desk to avoid the inevitable explosion, only he wouldn't fit. Her breasts rose and fell in her fury, fists curled at her sides. Jesus, she looked gorgeous when she got worked up. "Go ahead and return the money, you moronic asshole. I'm going to use it to erect a statue in Times Square. A hundred-foot, bronze middle finger pointing toward Queens."

Brent couldn't help it. He pushed her further. His anger

outweighed his common sense. And his libido crushed them both. Pissed-off Hayden equaled rough, dirty sex and he needed the release. The distraction. The idea of losing himself in her tempted him beyond control. "If you need a reminder of how much you enjoy my middle finger, just ask. You don't have to go building memorials in its honor."

She shook her head slowly. "This has all been one huge mistake."

No. No, that's not the reaction he'd wanted. He wanted her to throw him on the bed and ride out her temper. But she was already striding back into her room, steps clipped and purposeful. "Where are you going? This isn't over."

"It was over before it began." Brent caught up with her, but she jerked away when he grabbed her arm. Her rejection didn't deter him. *Wouldn't* deter him. Boosting her onto the waist-level dresser, he moved between her thighs and went to kiss her hard. As his mouth descended, her look of undiluted panic confused him and he paused. Words escaped her mouth in a rush. "Yes, I paid the tuition. It was nothing to me. *Nothing.* I'll spend that amount on hair product this month alone." She averted her eyes. "Get off me. When I decided I wanted a kept man, this isn't what I had in mind."

Hayden used Brent's shock as an opportunity to grab her overnight bag and dart out of the room.

Chapter Sixteen

Hayden walked slowly down Riverside Drive, grateful to finally be home, but unable to pick up the pace. Her limbs were sore, her brain fried. After sending a quick text to Story, she'd taken a cab from the Borgata to the Atlantic City Bus Terminal and ridden it back to Manhattan alone. Riding in the car with Brent had seemed too daunting in light of what happened. She knew her friend was probably a wicked combination of worried and curious, but she didn't have the energy to think about the inevitable conversation they had coming.

The two-hour ride would have been a good opportunity to think, if there hadn't been two teenage girls in front of her discussing cell phone upgrades. Or a man behind her reading every road sign they passed out loud, then translating it into French. She had, however, managed to come to one rock-solid conclusion. Her mother was smarter than she'd given her credit for. Obviously, she'd been paying closer attention than Hayden realized. She'd even handed the ammunition to her mother on a silver platter during their last phone call.

Actually, he's working two jobs because he helps support his brother's family. Plus, his sister in college. Which is kind of… well, it's pretty damn amazing.

What better way to ensure her and Brent's relationship tanked than hitting a man like him right where it hurts? Belittling his hard work. Cutting down his pride. Her mother's ploy worked like a charm. Brent hated her now. After everything, after she'd opened up to him, exposed herself in his arms, he still thought her presumptuous, thoughtless enough to pay his sister's college tuition. That he could think her capable of such a move for even a second made her cringe.

She hadn't denied it. If she could go back and have the confrontation again, she still wouldn't. What did it matter? His perception of her would never change, and trying to convince him otherwise would be exhausting and pointless. And it hurt. His judgment *hurt*.

It seemed his loathing of her lifestyle had done nothing to deter his attraction to her, however. He'd nearly taken her one last time on the hotel room dresser. Without question, if he'd kissed her, if she'd let his lips reach hers, she would have let him. Would have had no choice but to cling to him and accept the pleasure. She'd had no other option but to deliver a parting shot that would give her enough time to escape, because her attraction to him hadn't dimmed either. Not even slightly. The more distance the bus had put between them, she'd slowly recognized the attraction went far beyond their amazing sexual connection. She'd been so sure they'd found some common ground. So positive they were moving past their differences. Then he'd thrown it right back in her face.

Despite it all, despite everything, she missed him already. Still, maybe her mother had done her a favor by paying Lucy Mason's tuition on the sly and pinning it on her. If one misunderstanding was all it took to bring them back to an enemy state, they'd already been doomed.

Hayden glanced across the street toward her parents' brownstone and pulled up short when she saw her father standing outside, staring up at the structure. She waited for traffic to pass then crossed the street, her overnight bag growing heavy at her side.

"Dad? Are you locked out or something?"

He turned to her, still appearing lost in thought. His eyes, normally sharp and full of humor, were tired. A little dazed. "Oh hey, sweetheart. No, I'm not locked out." He gestured limply toward the house. "I just never really take the time to appreciate…what we have. Things, you know. We take them for granted until…" He trailed off.

She studied his face closely, guilt soaring through her. Her father's company, their family's livelihood, was at stake and she could think of nothing but her sore heart. Perhaps Brent was right and she was nothing but an overindulged brat. "Dad…I…"

He interrupted her. "I know your mother told you about our financial issues. I also know what she asked you to do. We had quite an argument about it, I'm afraid." Suddenly focused, his gaze found hers. "I don't want you to marry someone you don't love. I'd never ask that of you. Never."

Hayden swallowed heavily, unable to tell him she'd already decided against marrying Stuart. Afraid of his reaction to her selfish choice. "I know that. I know you wouldn't ask. Mother, however…" She got the desired laugh. "Not quite so accommodating."

"This is true." He shifted, digging his hands into his pockets. "Look, your mother doesn't have much faith in me. God knows I'm not cut out for this business. But I'm doing everything I can to resolve this without taking such…extreme measures."

She appealed to him with her eyes. "Dad, I'm asking you to please use the money you set aside in my name."

He was already shaking his head. "Never. Look, sweetheart. I'm working on it. Okay?"

Hiding her uncertainty, she squeezed his arm. "I know you are. Everything is going to work out fine, one way or another." He smiled warmly to acknowledge her support, but something just beyond her shoulder caught his attention. Tentatively, he raised his hand to wave at an approaching man in a suit. Hayden turned to him. "Who is that?"

Her father cleared his throat. "A Realtor. He's just here to appraise the house. No big deal." He looked away. "Just in case we can't find someone else to cover the loan in time."

"Is there zero chance Stuart will pay it?" She swallowed the knot in her throat. "Even without me marrying him?"

"He already paid it," her father murmured, distracted by the approaching man. He seemed to realize his slip then and scrambled to cover it. "That is to say, he paid it, then took it back. It was just one of those thin—"

"When?" She felt a rushing in her ears, as the complete puzzle began to form. "When did he take back the money?"

Her father's weary gaze dropped to the sidewalk. "Wednesday morning."

The morning after the dinner party. The morning after she'd flaunted another man in his face.

"Why?" Hayden whispered the question, even though the answer was devastatingly obvious. Stuart had bailed out her father, but she'd screwed them all over by bringing Brent to Stuart's house in some misguided act of rebellion.

"Your mother...she might have implied to Stuart that you were amenable to the marriage, so he paid the loan as a show of faith." He lifted a hand and let it drop limply to his side. "I'm sorry, Hayden. I didn't know." With a deep breath, he gripped her shoulder. "Listen, just try to trust me here. I'm working on fixing what I broke."

Hayden stood frozen on the sidewalk, watching her

father disappear into the house with the smiling man wearing a Bluetooth, his shoulders more hunched than usual. As if the weight of the world rested on his shoulders. He'd had that burden eased when Stuart paid off the loan, but her actions had thrust it back onto him. In that moment, she saw the harsh reality of her unorthodox family's situation. Before, it had only been a far-off possibility in her mind, but as she'd just witnessed, the end was far more imminent than she'd thought. Her dear father, for all his good intentions, wouldn't be able to stop the inevitable. The man who'd taken them in, given them everything they could ask for, would lose the home he'd known for decades. The house she'd grown up in. All of a sudden, her mother's meddling didn't seem so unnecessary. Selling the house would only be the tip of the iceberg. What about everything inside? Their lives would change drastically. And she could prevent it.

No, she *would* prevent it.

This was her chance. To finally repay her father for everything. To prove her worth. Brent had called her selfish. Perhaps he was right. Wouldn't it be selfish to let her family suffer when she had the means to stop it? She'd never earned this life. It had been given to her. If she stood by and watched her father be stripped of possessions he'd graciously shared with her, she'd never forgive herself.

Five minutes later, she walked through the front door of her town house. Story stomped out into the foyer on her cell phone, irritation radiating from every inch of her.

"She's here. Yes, she's fine, but not for long." Story hung up the phone. "Are you kidding me, dude? You text me with 'I hear Greyhound buses are lovely this time of year' and then vanish? Since when do you take the bus? Oh my God…you have amnesia, don't you?" She crept forward. "Hayden, it's me, Story."

"Who was on the phone?"

"Brent." When the device in question rang again, she hit ignore and shoved it into her jean shorts pocket. "And while we're on the subject of Mr. Mason…anything you want to talk about?"

"Yeah. You want to be the witness at my wedding tomorrow?"

"Damn, Brent works fast." Story laughed uncomfortably when Hayden didn't react to her joke. "Why don't you wait a few months and we can have a double wedding? We can get matching hairstyles."

Hayden burst into tears.

"Okay, okay. We'll wear light-up tiaras, too." Story wrapped her arms around Hayden and led her into the living room. "Come on, honey. I have a feeling this talk is long overdue."

"Liquor." She sucked in a breath. "I need liquor."

"That's a given."

. . .

Brent stood just inside Quincy's, waiting for his to-go lunch. Matt stood propped against the wall to his left, *both* of them silent for once as they nursed Coca-Colas. Hoping to get some decent advice, he'd asked Matt to meet him there, but now he had nothing to say. It hurt to talk. Every joke sounded cheap and hollow to his ears. Every word reminded him of the spectacular shit-show the weekend had turned into. How badly he'd handled the confrontation with Hayden, severing the fragile tether between them with his big, stupid mouth. Pushing her until she'd been forced to hit him with that knockout punch. *A kept man*. Shit. A day later it still stung.

Then she'd gone and disappeared, driving him out of his mind with worry and hitting home just how hard he'd actually fallen for her in the process. If he'd had time to cool off after Lucy's phone call, even just ten damn minutes, he might have been rational enough to communicate like a mature human being why her actions bothered him. Maybe right now he wouldn't be sitting in a shit-stew of physical and mental fuckery. He could be sneaking a call to her on this lunch break, making plans to see her later, instead of waiting on notoriously overcooked French fries in silence with Matt. Not that he didn't appreciate the company. He did. He'd just rather be talking to Hayden.

Now that he'd had a sleepless night and an equally shitty morning to replay yesterday's scene in his mind, over and over, he kept stumbling on little roadblocks. Hayden's confused reaction. The fact that paying Lucy's tuition didn't even feel like something she would do in the first place. The hurt on her face when he'd verbally cut down the bridge they'd managed to build over their differences. He loved their differences. Surprisingly, when it came right down to it, he didn't care that she had a lot of money. She could be as rich as two Oprahs and his feelings would remain the same, because *she* would still be the same. He'd never be a big enough man to accept charity, but if accepting the differences in their bank accounts meant being with Hayden, the decision was a no-brainer. He wanted *her*.

For so long, he'd been written off as the wiseass in their group of friends. The one everyone counted on to make the dirty joke. The one everyone rolled their eyes at. Hayden saw more. She saw the man who relished his responsibility to his family. The man whose job didn't make him insane, it made him committed. He'd even let down his guard in front of Daniel in Atlantic City thanks to Hayden's influence. She made him better. She made him see that more was possible.

Convincing her to give him another chance would be a feat, especially after yesterday when he'd wasted no time in highlighting every reason they couldn't work instead of all the reasons they *would* work. Off-the-charts sexual chemistry aside, he suspected they had more in common than either of them realized. They both loved a good fight. They showed one side of themselves to the world, keeping their compassion and vulnerabilities just under the surface. Family, duty, and responsibility meant everything to them both, even if their methods were vastly different. And hell...she fit right into his arms like she'd been molded for his body alone. He'd spent one night with her tucked against him and he was already ruined.

She'd talked about cannoli in her sleep. How ridiculously cute was that?

Oh God. He'd hurt the feelings of a girl who talked about cannoli in her sleep. The girl who'd tucked her feet between his legs to warm her toes. The girl who woke up smiling in his bed. He'd seen her in the mirror along the wall and it had nearly burst his chest wide open. He'd actually *hurt* that girl.

Okay. Don't panic yet. He'd get through his shift and go see her. Apologizing to her voice mail and moping around like a heartsick Jolly Green Giant wouldn't cut it any longer. He'd sit on her stoop and refuse to leave until she heard him out. Wasn't that what Troy had done with Ruby? Brent checked his watch. Six hours. He had six hours to figure out the right words. The ones that would convince her to give him a chance. Give *them* a chance. It wouldn't be easy, but he'd use everything in his arsenal.

"Hey, you know a good place to get roses around here? Not the cheap kind, like at the drugstore. Like, some legitimate roses that'll make it through the night."

Matt raised an eyebrow. "That's it? You've been standing there thinking for twenty minutes and your big epiphany is *roses*?"

"Really *nice* roses." Brent rolled his shoulders. "It's just a start. She probably won't even notice them, she'll be so dazzled by my eloquent speech."

"Is that so?"

"No." Brent dropped his head onto his hands. "I'm fucked."

After a moment, Matt sighed. "Listen, just be honest with her. Don't make any excuses for whatever jackass move you pulled. Sometimes all they need to hear is sorry." He sipped his drink. "It's a classic male move. Leaving out the sorry."

"Who *are* you?"

Matt shrugged, not answering.

"How do you know so much about what women want to hear?"

A beat passed. For the first time since Brent had known Matt, his unruffled demeanor slipped and something akin to pain shone through. "Sometimes we find out these things too late. Don't make that mistake." He cleared his throat and shifted in his seat, signaling the end of that particular topic. Brent reined in his curiosity and let it go without comment.

"All right. Any other advice, oh wise one?"

"Beg like hell." Matt gave a quick shake of his head. "I don't have a lot of experience with girls like Hayden. She's an incredibly sexy girl—"

"Bro."

He held up a hand. "Don't worry, my tastes are… different. However, she's the only girl I've come across who is remotely capable of putting up with your bullshit. No offense. I mean that in the nicest possible way."

"None taken." Brent crossed his arms. "You're right. I'm a dick."

"I wouldn't go that far." Matt sighed. "Actually, I take it back. I would go that far."

"Thanks, buddy."

"Any time." They both turned as Daniel walked into Quincy's. Looking highly preoccupied, he didn't see them until Brent put his fingers in his mouth and whistled. He leaned against the wall beside Brent and nodded at them, but didn't speak. Just stood there, twisting the engagement ring on his finger. Brent and Matt shared a look.

"Hey Danny, you missed it. Matt here just broke his record for consecutively spoken words. Giving advice, no less."

No response from Daniel.

"Seriously, if I'd closed my eyes, it would have been like Dr. Phil was standing right next to me."

Still nothing.

"All right, what's up with you, man?"

Daniel blew out a breath. "I don't know. Something was off with Story this morning. Have you spoken to Hayden?"

"Nope. And thanks for rubbing it in."

"She wouldn't even look at me before she left for work and now she's not answering her phone."

"It's nothing," Matt insisted. "You guys are solid. Stop overanalyzing."

Brent smiled. "See? Dr. Phil without the goofy accent."

Daniel grabbed Brent's Coke and took a healthy swallow. "Yeah...yeah, you're probably right." Before the words left his mouth, a phone rang and Daniel all but gave himself whiplash trying to extricate the source of the noise from his pocket. "It's her."

Matt and Brent rolled their eyes.

"Hey, sunshine." He listened silently for long moments, his skin growing pale. Brent could practically hear Story's frantic voice through the phone and frowned. Something was definitely wrong. His whole body tensed as Daniel met his eyes. Whatever had gone wrong, Hayden was involved. Jesus. How bad could it be? When Story finally paused, Daniel's responded very quietly. "Okay, listen to me, baby. You need to stall. Do whatever you have to do. Just don't let it happen."

He hung up.

Brent swallowed. "What is it?"

"We need to get down to City Hall."

A moment later, Brent burst through the front entrance of Quincy's and ran full speed for the ESU truck, Daniel and Matt right behind him.

Chapter Seventeen

Hayden and Story sat side-by-side on a hard wooden bench outside the city clerk's chamber, waiting for Hayden's turn to get married. She'd gone with a simple navy pencil skirt and white blouse. Her mother's pearl earrings. In clear protest of her decision, Story had shown up in frayed, cutoff jean shorts and moccasins. Last night, amid a sea of Chinese food containers and empty wine bottles, with *Troop Beverly Hills* playing in the background, she'd confessed everything to Story. Her friend's reaction had been as expected, simultaneously sympathetic and outraged, but she'd managed to exact her promise to keep quiet about Hayden's impromptu wedding.

After speaking with her father, she'd rushed to Stuart's apartment before any more damage could be done, negotiating his reinstatement of the loan payment in exchange for her promise to marry him the following day. To his credit, he hadn't made her grovel, even though he'd been decidedly smug. Just before she'd left, he'd asked her about Brent.

He's a nonissue, she'd said, nearly choking as she said the words.

Stuart, who stood several feet away, wore a perfectly tailored suit. Unfortunately, it only made her think of the king-size suit she'd rented for Brent. How amazing it had looked on him. And off of him. With a gulp, she tried to think of something—anything—else besides the man who'd barged his way past her defenses. Twenty-four hours ago, she'd been in bed with him. Hope burgeoning in her chest, along with a sense of rightness. Yesterday morning felt like it had taken place a decade ago, even if the pain of walking away from him was still horribly fresh.

Her fiancé laughed into his cell phone and checked his watch for the third time in as many minutes. He had a meeting to get to, after all.

Whoever said romance is dead?

"You don't have to do this," Story whispered to Hayden, blue-green glare fixed on Stuart. Having just met Hayden's future husband for the first time, Story had taken an immediate dislike to him. A rarity for her amiable best friend. Hayden didn't blame her. "There has to be another solution. I mean, my God, you're not some…sacrificial lamb. This is archaic."

"Did you come up with that line in the bathroom just now?"

"Yes. Did it work?"

Hayden patted her hand. "Sorry, Shakespeare."

Story sighed. "I know you were in no mood to discuss the elephant in the room last night"—she dropped her voice—"but *come on*. What about Brent?"

"He's more of an ape. And I'm still in no mood."

"Too bad," Story snapped, making Hayden's eyes widen. "There is something between you two. What do you think he would say if he was standing right here? If he knew you were about to marry someone else?"

She swallowed hard. *Don't think about it.* "He'd probably

say 'What are you doing *here*? The shoe sale is two blocks over!' Then he'd walk away, knuckles dragging on the ground."

"You don't believe that."

"The knuckles part?"

"All of it." Story pushed to her feet and started to pace just as a happy-looking couple emerged from the clerk's chamber. Their parents followed behind them taking pictures. Tears pricked Hayden's eyelids. Her parents wouldn't even be at her wedding. When she'd gone to Stuart yesterday afternoon and agreed to marry him, she'd done it on the condition that he leave her father in the dark. She didn't want him finding out before it was finished or he'd try to stop it. Her mother, on the other hand, seemed satisfied with this turn of events and was presently making sure her father stayed occupied until the deed was done.

"Stuart Nevin and Hayden Winstead," a court officer called from the chamber door, signaling their time had come. For a moment, she felt rooted to her seat, the pit in her stomach too heavy for her to move. Breathing steadily in and out through her nose, she stood on shaky legs and approached the chamber. She glanced over at Story, who chewed her lip as she followed them inside.

"Last chance, Hay," she whispered. "Say the word and we're out of here. I'll have us riding donkeys in Mexico by tomorrow morning."

Hayden gave a sad laugh. "I know you would, sweetie, and I love you for it." When Story barely bit back a sob, the pit in her stomach yawned wider. She attempted a brave face even though she felt her world caving in around her. "Hey, none of that. We can still ride donkeys in Mexico. This isn't going to change anything."

Story looked her square in the eye. "It's going to change *you*, Hayden."

Hayden's mouth dropped open, but no response came out. What could she say? Story was 100 percent right. A loveless marriage, a lifetime spent putting on a happy face, would kill her emotionally. She'd become just like every other bored and miserable high-society mama in Manhattan. Trying to fill the void with possessions.

Brent. What would become of him? He'd meet some spunky, outdoorsy-type with cute freckles she secretly hated. The kind of girl who would wear a Mets jersey and cheer like her life depended on every game's outcome. She'd probably say things like, "Let's grill out," and "Grab me a beer, hon?" She'd probably love camping and *The Three Stooges*. He'd have her knocked up with Brent Junior before the icing dried on their wedding cake. Her name would be Becky or Beth or Betsy and she'd wear his shirts to sleep at night.

Not fair! I want to wear his stupid, bigfoot-size shirts to sleep. Just thinking about Becky/Beth/Betsy and their Brent Brood made her so depressed, she was surprised to find herself still standing. Just as surprising, the clerk was already halfway through the marriage vows. Panic set in. Oh God. It suddenly hit her what a huge step she'd agreed to take. Hayden's frantic gaze flew to Stuart, who was asking the clerk if he could speed along the process. Marry *this* guy and forgo any chance with Brent? She couldn't do it. Could she?

What about her parents? Without their dozen or so charities to run, she could put her college degree to use and find a job. They might not have the life they were accustomed to anymore, but they could be comfortable. She would make sure of it.

"Hayden Winstead, do you take Stuart Nevin to be your husband?"

She opened her mouth, *hell no* perched on the tip of her tongue, when everything happened at once. Story, after darting a nervous glance toward the closed chamber door, squeezed her eyes shut. And flashed her breasts at the clerk.

Then the pounding on the door began.

...

This can't be happening. I'm just having a nightmare. The nightmare of the century. No, it's real. Too real. Oh my God, please tell me I made it. Please. She's my girl. Mine. No, no, no. I need her.

Brent left his ESU truck parked haphazardly against the curb and sprinted up the steps to City Hall, lights flashing behind him and thunder roaring in his ears. He didn't remember much about the last ten minutes. The high-speed race to Lower Manhattan. He'd managed to process most of Daniel's rapid explanation of Hayden's reasons for getting married, courtesy of Story's phone call.

At first, he'd thought the whole thing was some horrible mistake. She wouldn't marry someone else. They'd had a fight, yes, but shit, when were they *not* fighting? He'd made it very clear yesterday morning that she belonged to him and no amount of fighting would change that. However, marriage to some slimy corporate prick would. Legally. The more words that had come out of Daniel's mouth from the passenger seat, the more Brent knew Hayden was *actually* getting married at that very moment.

Her halted speech on the boardwalk in Atlantic City had come back to him in startling clarity. *He didn't have to take me in. I kind of owe him for everything, you know? Even if it sometimes means I have to do things that are…difficult.*

Not this. Never this. His Hayden married to the man who'd refused to take no for an answer that night in the kitchen? His vision went red all over again. He needed to get to her. No matter what it took, he wouldn't let it happen. Jesus, if he'd even made it on time.

Matt and Daniel caught up with him at the entrance, thankfully having the presence of mind to flash their badges at the security guard. The guard eyed Brent warily and he knew he had to look like a man possessed. He felt like it, too. His heart pounded so loudly, he couldn't think straight. All he could see was Hayden with someone else's ring on her finger. In someone else's bed. Having someone else's children.

That thought chilled him to the bone. He increased the pace of his run, somehow processing the room number Matt shouted behind him. He rounded the corner and saw the massive, wooden double doors with the words CITY CLERK stenciled above them. They were closed. When he reached them, he yanked on the knob, shaking the doors on their hinges, but they were locked. Keeping him from Hayden. He searched around, frantically looking for a security guard.

"Open it!" all three men shouted at the same time, badges out, when they spotted one.

The tall, skinny guard went white, as if he'd just glimpsed hell. "I-I'm supposed to leave it locked during ceremonies." He dropped his key ring on the ground with a clatter and stooped to retrieve them, hands shaking. "They're almost done, though. Just another few minutes…"

Brent roared Hayden's name and began pounding on the door with heavy fists. A few minutes left? At this very moment, Hayden could already be gone from him forever. No, she couldn't be. He wouldn't accept it. Knowing Daniel and Matt were working on getting the guard to open the door, he did the only thing he could do. He tried to stop the wedding *through* the door.

"Hayden Winstead! Don't you dare! Don't you *dare* marry someone else. We will fix this, do you understand me? If it means I have to work ten jobs. Your family will be fine. You don't have to do this. Please, *please* don't do this." He banged his head against the door, grateful for the pain somewhere besides his heart. "I know I'm an asshole but I'm working on it. I'm sorry for what I said. So sorry. Hurting you…it might be the worst thing I've ever done, but I don't deserve this. *You* don't deserve this. If you marry him, Hayden, I won't recover. I only got to spend one night holding you, but it was enough to know I have to hold you every single night."

Brent waited for a moment, to see if he could hear anything on the other side of the door, but only silence greeted him. He felt a hand on his shoulder, but he shrugged it off. Couldn't focus on anything but getting through to her. "What do I need to do, baby? Do you want me to sing 'Wind Beneath My Wings'? I'll do it. I'll deafen everyone in this building if that's what you want." When the silence remained, Brent's head dropped against the door with a curse. "You're really going to make me do this, aren't you?"

Then he gave Bette Midler a run for her money.

• • •

Hayden stood stock-still, flanked by her mother and father, watching in fascination as Brent belted out the *Beaches* classic at the city clerk's door. The one she'd ran out of five minutes ago. Halfway through his impassioned speech, from which her pulse still raced like crazy, the security guard had relented and stepped forward to unlock the door. Matt, however, finally noticing her standing ten yards away, had held him off with a look, allowing her to stand there while Brent poured his heart out.

Seconds after Story's needless, yet effective, intervention, her father had come bursting through the chamber door. He'd actually managed to pull off a deal with a foreign investor to keep the company afloat. Her mother, realizing Hayden's marriage to Stuart was now unnecessary, had fessed up to her father and told him about Hayden's plan for the afternoon.

Thank goodness she'd already decided not to marry Stuart or they might have been too late with the news. And she would be hearing this perfectly, beautifully, uniquely Brent speech from the wrong side of the door.

Her heart thumped so hard, she put her hands on her chest as though she could keep it from bursting free. This rough-edged, dirty-talking, wisecracking giant was singing to her as though his life depended on it and she'd almost given up the chance to be with him. Relief, powerful and encompassing, rolled through her in waves, accompanied by regret. If she'd believed for one minute that Brent had married someone else, she'd be devastated. Hayden could only imagine how he felt at that moment, thinking she'd discarded him without a word. Guilt poked holes in her relief. She needed his arms around her. It's the only thing that would calm the riot of emotions. Reassure her that she'd avoided catastrophe.

"Brent." Her voice came out sounding like a croak, so she tried again. "*Brent.*"

He spun around, eyes moving over her in a panic. "Oh God. I'm too late," he said dazedly, then slumped hard against the door.

Pain twisted in her chest, her throat constricted. "No, you're not too late. I couldn't do it."

Brent's head jerked up. He looked as though he wanted to believe her, but was unable to see past his fear just yet. "Why? Why couldn't you do it?"

"You know why," Hayden whispered.

"I just sang the theme song from *Beaches*. Tell me anyway."

She swallowed hard, words eluding her. Nothing she said could compare to the heartfelt speech he'd delivered moments before. So she closed her eyes and spoke from the heart. "I want you to leave your socks on my floor." A breath shuddered out. "Not on Beth or Betsy or Becky's floor. I want you to teach me how to grill. That's something you do, right?

In parking lots before sporting events or...or something?" She shook her head, knowing she rambled. "I want to...I want to be the one who worries about you. When you're at work. I want to zone out while you talk about baseball."

When she opened her eyes, Brent stood right in front of her, throat working with emotion. "Duchess—"

She rushed to finish before his nearness overwhelmed her. "I know the money bothers you, but I can't do anything about it. It's not who I am, though. Just try and remember that."

"Baby—"

"I don't care if freckle-faced Betsy is better for you, either. She can't have you."

"Woman, would you let me speak?" He clasped her face in his hands. "I want everything that comes along with you. All of it. And I don't know who the hell Betsy is, nor do I care. I only leave my socks on *your* floor. You're the only one who will ever have the right to worry about me. Or start an argument with me before breakfast." He ran a thumb across her bottom lip. "But I'm not letting you near the grill, darlin'. That there's a man's job."

Hayden launched herself into his arms with a laugh. Everything in the world felt right again when he wrapped them around her and swayed on his feet. She pressed her face against his strong neck. "I'm sorry. I'm sorry. I didn't think I had a choice."

"You did. You made the right one." He pulled back to kiss her forehead, her cheeks. "The two of us can figure this out. I won't let you be sorry for choosing me."

She couldn't speak for a moment as she regarded the man in front of her. He would do it, too. Help her support her family without a word of complaint. This goofy, loving, incomparable man. "I could never be sorry for that." She nodded toward her father. "But fortunately that won't be the case. Dad came through in the clutch."

Her father's eyes sparkled as he stepped forward to shake Brent's hand, Hayden's mother at his side, arms crossed. "I was coming here to stop a wedding. Turns out I didn't need to. She ran out of there like a bat out of hell."

Brent squeezed her to his side and smiled at her mother. "Mrs. Winstead."

"Mother, do you have something you'd like to tell Brent?"

Primly, she raised her chin. "I apologized already to Hayden for going behind her back to pay your sister's tuition. I don't see why I have to do it twice."

Brent flinched at her mother's words and pulled her closer. "I'm an asshole for assuming. Working on it," he whispered in her ear.

"Mother," Hayden prompted.

"Oh all right. My apologies." She perused her nails. "I won't pretend I'm heartbroken over losing Stuart as a son-on-law. Bit of an ass, isn't he?"

Laughing, they both started to respond, when Daniel snagged their attention. "I'm sorry to interrupt. Where is Story?"

Hayden disengaged from Brent's side and laid a gentle hand on Daniel's arm. "Now I don't want you to overreact—"

As if on cue, two security guards emerged from the office behind Daniel, flanking a handcuffed Story. Daniel froze, face losing all color. "What the hell is going on here?"

"She flashed the city clerk," the guard explained, looking bored.

"What?"

Story winced at his tone. "You told me to stall," she called over her shoulder as they dragged her down the hallway. "Don't tell my dad, okay?"

After a moment of stunned disbelief, Daniel ran after them. "Hey! Uncuff her! That's my girlfriend."

"Fiancé, Daniel."

They disappeared around the corner. Matt followed after them muttering something about needing to find new friends. Hayden, knowing Daniel would never let Story get taken away in a police car, finally relaxed. The minutes before Brent arrived had been spent haggling with the guards and calling her parents' various lawyer friends on Story's behalf.

She took Brent's arm and pulled him aside. Her parents seemed to sense they wanted some privacy and followed in their friends' wake. They were finally alone.

"Aren't you going to—"

"*Yes*," Brent growled, capturing Hayden's mouth with his own. Her lips parted on a gasp and his tongue swept inside, possessing her. Reminding them both that she belonged to him. Reminding her who made her body weak and strong at the same time. She sensed that after the morning they'd had, he needed reassurance, and was only too happy to provide it. His hands cupped her elbows to drag her up against him. When he leaned in to reclaim her mouth a second time, she pulled back just a little, then took control of the kiss. A reminder that he belonged to *her*, too. She buried her fingers in his hair and slanted her mouth over his, again and again, until he broke away with a choked sound.

"I'm in charge every night for the next week. No exceptions."

Hayden nipped at his chin. "I'm going to make you work for it."

He caught her up in his arms, long strides carrying them toward the exit. "Woman, I'm counting on it."

Epilogue

Brent looked up from the explosives and demolitions handbook he'd been studying, smiling when he heard Hayden's keys jingle outside the front door of her town house. Knowing she expected him to be waiting on the other side filled him with a now-familiar sense of calm. The way they'd come to depend on each other, trust each other, never failed to humble him. Every night she walked through the front door, searching for him with those beautiful eyes, felt like the first time. But he wanted tonight to be special.

She walked in a second later, looking polished and professional in her black skirt and heels. Stockings, as well. Always the damn stockings. Six months earlier, she'd gone to work for her father's firm, reinvigorating the charity branch with a determination he'd come to expect and admire in her. Turns out, his girl was a straight-up shark, bringing in donors left and right, not only for the Clear Air program, but new charities she'd initiated in the company name. Those nights, when she came over, all flushed with pleasure after landing a new sizable donation…God, he looked forward to those nights. He looked forward to *every* night with her, but being the recipient of all that passion humbled him. In addition to turning him on like nobody's business.

Yes, she might dress the part of a corporate player, but he knew the girl just beneath the cool surface. The girl who made him laugh, surprised him every day…the girl who kept him awake at night thinking of ways to make her happy. They spent most evenings at his place in Queens. She'd become a permanent fixture at dinner and on the weekends. He'd started dropping hints months ago that he wanted her there permanently. First, he'd given her keys, with a mini high-heel keychain. Then he'd asked for Laurie's help redecorating to make the house more "chick-friendly." Not only for Hayden, but because his sister Lucy was due home in a week from graduate school. Finally, he'd asked Hayden one night as they were cooking dinner and she'd promised to think about it.

When he'd arrived at her place tonight, he'd seen the appraisal of her town house from the Realtor pinned to her refrigerator. Her simple but effective way of telling him yes. He'd been thankful to be alone in that moment. No sense in letting her know what a sap he turned into.

Until now, her town house had been mostly reserved for hot, stolen lunch hours when they could both swing it. That's when, thanks to their new appreciation for role-play, things tended to get kinky. His pulse tripped over itself in anticipation. He'd come to her place tonight since she'd been forced to work through her lunch hour today. He was simply too impatient to wait the forty-five minutes it took her to get to Queens.

Their eyes met across the living room and he watched Hayden go soft, her body relax, as she saw him, making his heart pound even harder. True to her word, she worried about him. At first, he'd thought it unnecessary, but damn if he didn't love the way she breathed a sigh of relief every day when she saw him. She set her briefcase down on the kitchen table and removed her jacket. When she started toward him, he shook his head.

"Uh-uh. Stay right there."

Brent had the pleasure of watching awareness leap into her gaze, her chest rising and falling with soft breaths as she watched him approach. When he slipped the handcuffs from his pocket and let them dangle between them, she wet her lips, eyes seeming to momentarily lose focus. He loved having that effect on her. "What did I do, Officer?"

"I'll tell you when I'm damn well ready." The second he had her within reaching distance, he spun her around until she faced the table. Then in a move guaranteed make her damp, he reached beneath the hem of her skirt and shoved her knees wide. Without an ounce of gentleness. Slapping the cuffs onto her wrists, he savored her aroused whimper, letting it go to his head and elevate him to that incredible place only Hayden could. He leaned over her back to breathe his words against her ear. "Did you really have to work through lunch? Or did you just want to make me wait? Make me suffer?"

"I don't know what you're talking about."

His deep laugh coincided with her shiver. "Oh no?" Brent curled his fingers under the material of her skirt and dragged it up slowly, over her smooth ass, unable to wait a second longer to reveal her sexy backside. He pushed her upper body forward until her cheek rested on the table and he could savor the sight of her bent over in front of him. Beautiful flesh greeted him at the tops of her stockings; the swath of black material running between her thighs caused his erection to press painfully against his zipper. He held her still, looking his fill until she started to writhe, then he unzipped his pants with one hand, communicating with a tightening of his hold that she wasn't to move. When he'd finally freed himself with a relieved groan, he ran a knuckle up the center of her panties.

"I don't mind waiting for it, baby. In fact, I love it." He tugged her panties down her legs. "It means you want to be fucked twice as hard."

"Yes," she moaned. "Please, Officer. As hard as you can."

Brent began to sweat. Jesus, she knew exactly what to say to make him crazed to be inside her. Still, as much as he loved the game, he wanted to see his Hayden. Needed to connect with her in that indescribable way. Especially tonight.

He gently turned her around and planted her ass on the kitchen table. Looking her in the eye, watching her read his mind, he sank two fingers deep inside her.

She sucked in a breath. "Hello to you, too."

His mouth took hers in a long, wet kiss, rife with promises. "I'm feeling a little impatient, duchess," he said against her mouth. "Are you wet enough or do you want my tongue?"

In response, she parted her thighs in welcome, her hot gaze on his arousal, as if imagining how she would touch him if her hands were free. But they weren't. Which turned them both on even more. Brent yanked her closer to the edge of the table, not bothering to settle between her legs, but rocking against her as soon as he made contact. Automatically they circled his waist and squeezed, urging him to move faster. Their moans echoed in the silent room. "You're impatient, too. I feel your thighs shaking around my hips already."

"Maybe I'm cold."

"You're never anything but fucking hot."

Hayden's mouth beckoned to him, begging for a long, wet kiss. Brent accommodated her, groaning as her high heels dug into the flesh of his ass as he worked himself against her core. "Aren't you going to ask me about my day?" she asked breathlessly. He mumbled an incoherent response into her mouth. "I landed a new account at work. You know what that means."

Brent pulled back, his lips curling into a smile. He

watched her closely, loving the way her mouth parted in pleasure as he picked her up off the table and sank back onto a dining room chair. When the position drove him even deeper, they both moaned, Hayden beginning to roll her hips immediately. Knowing he was seconds from being ridden hard and rendered speechless, Brent took one last pull off her mouth and said the words that had been racing through his head for weeks. "Hayden." He waited until her eyes focused on him. "Marry me, baby."

For a moment that seemed to stretch for eternity, she looked stunned and out of breath. "You wait until I'm cuffed to propose?"

He ran unsteady hands up her smooth thighs. "When have we ever done anything the conventional way?"

"Never. Thank God." The corners of her lips edged up, hips beginning to move once more in a devastating rhythm. "Now ask me again. Nicely."

He surged up from the chair, and Hayden's gasp of surprise tasted sweet on his tongue as he strode toward the bedroom. "You forgot who's wearing the cuffs, duchess."

Acknowledgments

To my husband, Patrick, and daughter, Mackenzie, whom I adore beyond words…

To Heather Howland for loving these characters as much as I do…

To Liz Pelletier for providing such valuable insight on the "enemies to lovers" trope…

To Tahra Seplowin for being a rock star and an excellent brunch companion…

To my cousins J & J for teaching me that an insult can be the most sincere expression of love…

To all the amazing readers of the Line of Duty series and my fabulous Babes…

Thank you, thank you, thank you.

About the Author

NYT and *USA TODAY* bestselling author Tessa Bailey lives in Brooklyn, New York, with her husband and young daughter. When she isn't writing or reading romance, she enjoys a good argument and thirty-minute recipes.

www.tessabailey.com
Join Bailey's Babes!

Discover the Line of Duty series…

PROTECTING WHAT'S HIS
HIS RISK TO TAKE
OFFICER OFF LIMITS
STAKING HIS CLAIM
PROTECTING WHAT'S THEIRS

Also by Tessa Bailey

UNFIXABLE
BAITING THE MAID OF HONOR
OWNED BY FATE
EXPOSED BY FATE
DRIVEN BY FATE
RISKIER BUSINESS
RISKING IT ALL
UP IN SMOKE
CRASHED OUT
BOILING POINT
RAW REDEMPTION
THROWN DOWN
WORKED UP
WOUND TIGHT

Enjoy more heat from Entangled...

PLAYING IT TOUGH
a Sydney Smoke Rugby novel by Amy Andrews

Cosmetic tattoo artist Orla Stewart went from being the ultimate party animal to living a life that's ridiculously straight and narrow. Turns out, cancer can change a girl. A lot. Until one very hot, very unwelcome intruder turns things upside down. American rugby import Ronan Dempsey needs to clean his act up, and the pool house belonging to a family friend is the perfect place to hideaway. The chemistry is instantaneous, charged, and absolutely, completely, totally off-limits. Now it's a deliciously torturous game of pushing boundaries and holding out. It's just a matter of time before someone breaks…

A SWEET SPOT FOR LOVE
a novel by Aliyah Burke

Former pro baseball player Linc Conner knows exactly where his head's at. But when it comes to single mom Emma Henricksen, Linc can't see straight. Emma's too busy raising her gifted little girl to have a sex life that's not battery-operated. Still, how could she resist being engaged to a guy who's the sexual equivalent of her favorite dessert, even if it's just pretend? Now it's a game with a whole lot of chemistry between the guy who's used to playing the field—and the woman who opted out of the game long ago. All that's missing is one helluva curveball…

Printed in Great Britain
by Amazon